CRAZY ABOUT
THE BOSS

CRAZY ABOUT THE BOSS

BY

TERESA SOUTHWICK

First published in Great Britain 2006
Large Print edition 2007
Harlequin Mills & Boon Limited,
Eton House, 18-24 Paradise Road,
Richmond, Surrey TW9 1SR

© Harlequin Books S.A. 2006
Special thanks and acknowledgement are
given to Teresa Ann Southwick for her contribution to
The Brides of Bella Lucia series.

ISBN-13: 978 0 263 19444 9
ISBN-10:   0 263 19444 2

Set in Times Roman 17 on 22 pt.
16-0407-40300

Printed and bound in Great Britain
by Antony Rowe Ltd, Chippenham, Wiltshire

For the Romance readers—without you
there would be no happy endings!

PROLOGUE

New York—December 23

HEARING his sister's voice always made Jack feel like that eighteen-year-old who'd left home in disgrace.

How bloody stupid was that? He was Jack Valentine of Valentine Ventures, the reckless genius who had challenged conventional wisdom and made a fortune. And she was asking him to come home again.

Jack squeezed the phone until his fingers ached. "It's been twelve years, Emma. That's a lot of Christmases. Why should I come home for this one?"

"Do you have something better to do?" she said, her soft, cultured voice dripping with irritation.

A muscle jumped in his jaw. It was almost as if she knew he had no plans at all. "Anything's better than that."

"It's time, Jack."

He heard London in her voice. Americans loved the accent. But he heard silk and steel in the soft, firm tone that tapped into an accumulation of loneliness he hadn't realized was there.

Swiveling his chair around, he stared out his office window and concentrated on the New York skyline instead. It was dark, but across the city lights dotted the windows in the tall buildings. Out there someone was staring at *his* window and coveting this office with its expensive art, plush carpet, fine furniture and the latest electronics. Standing on the street they were cold and scared and staring, wondering what it felt like to have everything you ever wanted.

He knew because twelve years ago this city was where he'd run and he'd once been down there with nothing. He'd looked up and vowed that one day he'd own the whole damn building. Screw-ups didn't grow up to be millionaires, but he had.

"It *has* been twelve years, after all. Are you listening, Jack?"

"Yes. And what I hear is that something's wrong. What is it, Em?"

There was a big sigh from the other end of the line. "All right. There is a problem here. The business is in trouble. We need your help."

The precious business Robert Valentine prized above everything? Good. It was about time the womanizing bastard paid for his sins where it hurt him most. "I'm not sure why I should care."

"Because no matter how stubborn you insist

on being, you're still part of this family." This time censure mixed with the steel in her voice.

"Did he put you up to this?"

"No." Another big sigh. "Jack, what happened between the two of you?"

Jack had protected his mother. And it had cost him.

"It doesn't matter any more, Em."

The unladylike snort on the other end of the line told him his sister was probably rolling her pale blue eyes in disgust as she fiddled with a strand of curly light brown hair. The vivid image made him miss her.

"I hear in your voice that it still *does* matter," she said quietly.

"You're wrong. Now, if that's all—" He turned away from the window and leaned back in his chair.

"It's not," she snapped. "We need you, Jack. Your job is investing in companies. The family business needs money and quite literally you're our only hope to keep it going."

"Lots of investors would love to get their hands on a piece of the action."

"But they wouldn't be family. And none of us want to give a non-Valentine a piece of the action because you don't turn your back on family. It simply isn't right."

Even if family turned their backs on him? he wondered. "They'll survive, Em."

"I wish I could be as sure." Sadness shaded her voice. "As you said—it's been a dozen years. Twelve seems like a good round number to make peace. Tis the season. Peace on earth. Charity begins at home and all that."

"I'm not feeling charitable." Jack rested his elbows on his cluttered desk.

"Neither am I." Frustration laced with anger making her tone more clipped. "You disap-peared," she blurted out. "Dad wouldn't discuss it and Mum was fragile. I was sixteen when you left me with the whole mess. Big brothers are supposed to take care of their little sisters."

Little sister knew how to stick the knife in and twist. He'd loved her. Hell, he still loved her.

"I had no choice, Em. I had to leave."

"That doesn't change the fact that you abandoned me, but you did what you needed to, I guess. Now I need something from you." She hesitated a moment, then said, "I got married, Jack."

It took him two beats to pull himself out of the past. His little sister was a married woman? He hadn't heard. "Congratulations. Who's the lucky man?"

"He was a prince—"

"Of course he'd be a prince of a guy," he teased.

She laughed, a happy sound, so different from a few moments ago. "No, Sebastian was actually crowned King of Meridia."

Meridia. Jack knew it was a small European country and recalled something in the news recently about a scandal in the line of succession. "I've heard of it."

"It's very important to me that you meet him."

"Look, Emma—"

"I've never asked you for anything," she interrupted, her voice firm. "But I want this and, quite frankly, I think you owe me, Jack. Come for Christmas. The usual place for the family toast. I'll be expecting you."

Before he could decline again, the line went dead. Jack let out a long breath as he replaced the phone. His little sister married a king?

And he'd missed it.

That made him wonder what else he'd missed. But Emma had never told him that she'd felt abandoned. And she *hadn't* ever asked him for anything. Until now.

"Jack, you're out of your mind." His associate, Maddie Ford, walked into his office without looking up from the proposal he'd given her earlier. "You can't seriously want to put money into this. It's crazy. It's risky. And so like you it makes me want to shake you until your teeth rattle."

She kept talking, but he was only half listening to blonde, blue-eyed, brainy Maddie. His sensible and down-to-earth, tell-it-like-it-is Maddie. In the two years since he'd brought her into his company, she'd become more his partner than his assistant. He'd come to rely on her sound judgment. For better or worse she'd become the voice in his head.

She was also the only stunningly beautiful woman he'd never hit on. And he planned to keep it that way because the women who gave in to him were here today and gone tomorrow. Sometimes they were gone in the same day. He wouldn't do anything to lose Maddie because he needed her around, although what he had in mind wasn't business related. The thing was, he hadn't made a fortune by *not* listening to his gut and it was telling him now to take her with him to meet Emma's husband.

When she stopped talking to catch a breath he said, "How do you feel about Christmas in London?"

CHAPTER ONE

London—Christmas Day

"I SUPPOSE millionaires have problems, too."

Maddie Ford waited for a reaction from the bachelor millionaire in the town car beside her and Jack Valentine didn't disappoint.

He glared at her. "What's that supposed to mean?"

"I'm sorry. Did I say that out loud?" she asked, making her eyes as wide and innocent as she could manage.

"You know good and well you did. Was that a blonde moment? Don't go blonde on me now,

Maddie," he said, irritation in his voice. Or was it tension?

Definitely tension and that wasn't like Jack. Whatever business had made him insist she come along on this trip must be really important because the strain was showing.

And that was starting to concern her. Jack Valentine was rich, handsome, charismatic and often touted as New York's most eligible bachelor. He did the charming British thing with overtones of brash American and it worked way too well. From his short, black, carefully mussed hair to his dark blue eyes with the bad-boy gleam that promised trouble in a most appealing way, he exuded the same exciting vibes that had brought down her heart not once, but twice.

In the beginning, she'd had a crush on him but quickly learned he wasn't a one-woman man. So the fact that he'd never tried anything had convinced her she wasn't his type. He wasn't likely to turn his charm in her direction, which was just fine with her. She liked her job.

For the last two plus years she and Jack had worked well together. Her sensible side balanced Jack's tendency toward rashness. They had been a team. Until he'd messed with her Christmas plans. Although he hadn't smiled or teased her since leaving New York. The way he was acting made her feel guilty for giving him a hard time. Maybe a little teasing of her own could lighten him up because he normally didn't do tension.

"If by 'going blonde' you're referring to my current state of irritation, let me assure you I have a very good reason. It's Christmas. And I'm on the wrong continent. Is there a reason this trip couldn't have waited?"

"It's one day and I did promise to make it up to you."

That was a non-answer. "How do you make up for missing Christmas? I had plans."

"I know. You've made that quite clear."

He didn't need to know that her plans hadn't been with family. Her married siblings alternated holidays with their spouses' families and this year her parents had taken a cruise. They'd invited her because they felt sorry for their twenty-eight-year-old unmarried-and-not-dating daughter. She'd declined because it seemed too pathetic for words, but she hadn't shared any of that with Jack. He'd have teased her unmercifully and teasing from Mr Bachelor-about-town regarding her non-existent love life would be too humiliating.

"It's good of you—"

"No, it's not. I'm not good."

"Okay. You're bad. I can live with that." For a split second, he flashed his carefree, charming Jack Valentine grin.

Was his grin always that potent? Or did his uncharacteristic tension just make it seem more thrilling than usual? Not going there, she thought. "I can't believe you played the because-you're-the-boss card to get me here."

"Our difference of opinion showed no signs of letting up. In the interest of time, it seemed the expedient thing to do."

She'd disagreed because she hadn't liked his attitude and now it was time for his reminder that he couldn't walk all over her. "My being here makes no more sense now than it did before. Since when do you want me to come along? And what business couldn't wait a day? More important, who does business on Christmas? It's un-American."

"Then it's a good thing we're in Britain."

Did he just snap at her? That was out of character, too. But before she could demand to know what was going on with him, the car smoothly pulled to the curb in front of a restaurant. It was then she realized that by continuing their disagreement on a different continent, she'd missed seeing anything of London. It didn't matter that it was too dark to see all that much, she really wanted to see London. At least he'd promised her a couple days there. That had finally broken down her resistance.

"Why are we stopping here?" she asked.

"It's something I have to do." There was an edge to his voice that said whatever he had to do was tantamount to a firing squad at dawn.

There was an angry, dark look on his face that frightened her, mostly because she'd never seen it before. "What's going on, Jack?"

"I have to see my sister."

"Your sister?" If Maddie hadn't been so shocked, she'd have come back with a brilliantly clever retort. But she *was* shocked and said exactly what she was thinking. "I didn't know you had a sister."

"Well, now you do."

"What else don't I know?" she asked as the driver opened the door for them to get out.

A lot, Jack thought, and he ignored the question, as he didn't plan to enlighten her. He would see Emma and meet her husband. Duty fulfilled and he'd leave.

Cold London air filled his lungs as he slid out of the car before her. He walked slowly toward the Bella Lucia restaurant he hadn't been able to get out of fast enough twelve years ago. The gate he pushed open was familiar, as was the courtyard in front of the building. Small white lights twinkled in the shrubs and a subdued glow coming through the frosted windows pooled gold at his feet. There were people inside.

His family. And he was on the outside looking in, a thought that opened up an empty feeling deep inside him.

"Jack?"

He looked at Maddie, grateful for her

presence and determined not to let her know. It was just this once, because he wouldn't let himself need anyone.

"Let's get this over with," he said.

"Way to make me even more joyful about missing out on the biggest holiday of the year."

Her sarcasm made him smile. Brutal honesty was what he counted on from Maddie. She'd never been more indispensable to him than she was at this moment.

He pushed open the door, walked inside the restaurant and looked around. It was all different. Gone was the original Italian style and in its place was a trendy, smart, fashionable restaurant. A restaurant that went dead quiet as everyone turned and silently stared at him.

He recognized his uncle John, in the center of the room with glass in hand for the traditional holiday toast. Robert Valentine stood beside him and Jack met his father's gaze across the room. The rest of the family clustered on either side of the two men and looked from him to Robert. Jack would swear every last one of them were holding their breath. He could almost reach out and grab the friction out of the air.

Maddie leaned over. "They're all staring at us, Jack."

"I know."

"Do you realize everyone is looking at us as if I'm Scrooge and you're the Ghost of Christmas Past? Are we crashing a private party?"

"We are, yes."

Jack didn't take his eyes off his father. Every muscle in his body tensed as he waited for the man who'd sent him packing to make the first move. The young woman beside Robert looked anxiously between them and the seconds ticked off like the timer on an explosive device.

Finally she rushed over to him. "Jack, you came. I didn't think you would."

"Emma?" He recognized the voice, but the petite, curvy young woman in front of him had been a gawky sixteen-year-old when he'd left. Now she was glamorous and sophisticated, her hair no longer light brown, but blonde shot with honey-colored highlights. "You're all grown up."

"As are you. You're just in time for the family toast." She handed first him then Maddie a flute of champagne.

"Merry Christmas, everyone." His uncle John continued as if nothing out of the ordinary had happened. "Here's to a holiday season filled with health, happiness and success." He held up his glass. "To family."

Murmurs of agreement filled the room as everyone sipped from their crystal flutes. Without drinking, Jack set his glass on the white linen cloth covering the table beside him.

"Welcome home, Jack," Emma said, even as she frowned at the champagne he'd abandoned.

"This isn't my home."

And as soon as he met his sister's new husband, he and Maddie could get the hell out of here. He looked at her bright blonde hair and big blue eyes, letting himself feel the familiar tug for a beautiful woman. In her case he'd never given in to it because he respected her too much. She was different from the women he dated and his relationship with her was as sacred as the separation between church and state.

Emma ignored his sharp words as she looked at Maddie. "Who's this, then?"

"Madison Ford. I'm Jack's assistant." Maddie held out her hand. "Call me Maddie. Or better yet, Scrooge," she finished.

"No Christmas spirit?" Emma asked.

"I left it back in New York. I had plans."

"After you called," Jack said to his sister, "I

decided to move up a scheduled business trip and convinced Maddie to come along. Where's your husband?"

Emma turned to look, then smiled at the man just joining them. He stood military straight, even as he slid his arm around her waist. Not quite as tall as Jack, he had wavy dark hair and brown eyes.

Adoration shone on Emma's face as she leaned into the man. "His Highness Sebastian Marchand-Dumontier of Meridia meet Jack Valentine, my brother."

They shook hands and Jack noted the prince's firm grip. *Always squeeze a man's hand as if you mean it. No one respects you if your hand feels like a limp codfish.*

When his father's words flashed through his mind, Jack knew it had been a mistake to come. Then he looked at Maddie as the prince kissed her hand.

"It's a pleasure to meet you, Your Highness," Maddie said.

"Please, Sebastian is fine," he said graciously.

Maddie looked at Emma. "That would make you what? Queen? Princess Consort? I can never keep that straight."

"Emma will do," she said with a twinkle.

"Quite nicely," her husband added, smiling down at her.

Maddie was studying his sister. "I think there must be something in the royal rulebook about fabulous jewels. If you show me your tiara, it might almost make up for the fact that I'm missing Christmas in the States."

Laughing, Emma leaned into her chuckling prince. "I'm afraid the tiara's at home in Meridia's royal vault. But do come for a visit, Maddie. I've a feeling you and I would get on very well together."

"I'm not sure I could spare her," Jack cut in.

"I'd love to visit Meridia," Maddie countered, shooting him a look. "His Lordship will just have to get along without me."

"Jack."

He turned and recognized his older brother, Max, and pleasure shot through him. He put out his hand and Max took it, then the two of them grinned at each other.

Emma cleared her throat. "I'll let you and Max catch up, Jack."

"How long will you be in London?" Maddie asked her.

"We're on holiday for several weeks." She looked at Jack. "And you? How long will you be here? Are you planning to see Mum?"

"I hadn't thought about it," he said.

"You should." Emma stood on tiptoe and hesitated a moment before kissing his cheek. "You look well but not happy, Jack."

The casual comment brought the same rush of

emptiness that had washed over him when he'd looked through the window. Why now? He'd managed fine without them all these years, proving he didn't need them or anyone else.

"Not happy? And you can tell that in five minutes?"

"Less." She slid her hand into her husband's and their fingers intertwined. "Now that I know what happiness looks like, it's easy to see when it's not there. We'll talk later."

She and her husband walked away and mingled with the rest of the family. Then he looked at Max and felt again that soul-deep, overwhelming loneliness. They were half-brothers and had been best friends. Max had been the one to introduce him to parties, girls and fast cars.

Jack realized how much he'd missed him. "It's good to see you, Max."

"You, too." Max looked at Maddie. "Aren't you going to introduce me to your significant other?"

"I'm significant and Jack has many 'others', but I'm not one of them," Maddie retorted.

"Excellent news. I'm Max Valentine."

"Jack's brother?" she guessed.

"Indeed."

"Maddie Ford," she said. "Jack's assistant as opposed to his significant other. Upon occasion, to my dismay, I've dutifully smoothed the ruffled feathers of his significant others. Which I guess would then make them insignificant."

Max grinned. "You're a feisty one."

Jack was taken by surprise when an unreasonable flash of resentment ripped through him. "You're not her type, Max."

"How do you know?" she asked.

"Max actually has a personality."

Maddie finished off the champagne in her glass. "Then maybe I should get to know him and his personality better," she shot back.

Before Jack could figure out how he could be so pleased to see his brother at the same time he wanted to wring his neck for flirting with Maddie, his father joined them.

The older man rested his hand on his Max's shoulder. "And so," Robert Valentine said, "the prodigal son returns."

CHAPTER TWO

THE last time Jack had been face to face with his father, Robert Valentine had been enraged. Now he showed no emotion, not even surprise. He was still handsome, the silver flecks in his black hair giving him a distinguished look. His black eyes revealed nothing about his feelings for the son who had spent eighteen years trying to get his notice. The son who had struggled to control his natural enthusiasm. The son who now controlled the fate of this restaurant.

The irony of that almost made him smile.

Jack had literally looked up to his father twelve years ago, but now he looked him straight in the eye. He'd made himself a powerful man and was no longer that unsure boy who craved his father's good opinion.

"Hello, Dad."

"Jack." Robert smiled his practiced smile. "It's been a long time. To what do we owe this unexpected surprise?"

"Emma called."

Something flickered in Robert's eyes. "Did she now?"

"Yes. To tell me she got married."

"Did she say anything else?" A muscle jumped in his father's jaw.

In anyone else that tightening of the mouth would be nothing. For his stiff-upper-lipped father it signaled nervousness in the man Jack had once thought invincible. Satisfaction surged through Jack. If it made him a bastard that he took pleasure in the old man's problems, so be it.

"She said she wanted me to meet her husband," Jack answered.

"Sebastian. Nice chap."

Jack shrugged. "Hard to tell in a few minutes, but my sister seems happy."

"She's blossomed, our Emma has, into a beautiful, self-confident young woman."

"She has, yes."

Funny how leaving Robert Valentine's shadow had that effect.

"I hear you've done well for yourself, Jack," Robert said.

"Does that surprise you?"

Instead of answering, Robert turned his gaze to Maddie. "And who's this, then?"

She held out her hand. "Maddie Ford. Jack's assistant," she added before his father made the "significant other" assumption.

"Robert Valentine," he said, shaking her

hand. "It's a pleasure to meet you. Welcome to Bella Lucia."

"Thank you."

"Have you been to England before?"

She shook her head. "This is my first visit."

"And Christmastime in London is a fine introduction." Robert smiled at her.

"I have business," Jack said.

"I do hope work won't keep you from seeing some of London." His father's voice oozed charm.

"It won't. Jack promised." Maddie smiled brightly, a clear indication that the Valentine charm was working on her. "It would be a shame to come all this way and not take in the sights. Traveling has always been on my list of things to do."

"Don't put things off, Maddie," Robert warned, "All work and no play…"

Hypocritical bastard! Vibrating with anger,

Jack took a step forward and stopped inches from his father. "And how would you know about balancing work and play? For all the time you gave your family, we might have been pet frogs. When you weren't buried in work, you played with women who were not your wife."

Maddie put a hand on his arm. "Jack—"

He barely felt the touch, but her tone got his attention. The shocked expression on her face cleared the red haze of rage from his head. He blew out a long breath. "We're leaving, Maddie."

Shock turned to surprise and there were questions in her eyes. "But it's just been—"

"We can't stay," Jack interrupted.

Robert frowned. "You've come a long way. Surely you can have dinner—"

"We have other plans," he snapped.

Jack had come because of Emma, but he didn't owe this man a thing and this place held no good memories for him. Right here the world as he'd known it had come apart. He'd rebuilt his life, but no one would be that important to him again.

As Jack hustled Maddie back out into the cold he acknowledged irony for the second time and didn't appreciate it. Just like that night a dozen years ago, he couldn't get out of Bella Lucia fast enough.

The difference was that this time he was leaving with Maddie, the only woman he trusted.

After checking into a suite at Durley House, Maddie couldn't wait to get out of her travel clothes and into something more comfortable. If only she could get out of her thoughts as easily. The scene at Bella Lucia had really shaken her.

She'd never seen Jack like that. The repressed violence she'd felt in him had shocked her because she was accustomed to his easygoing charm, a trait she suspected he'd inherited from his father after meeting the man. This darker Jack with an aura of danger hanging over him was someone she didn't know at all. And she couldn't stop thinking about him.

She didn't like thinking about Jack outside of business because, by definition, outside of business meant personal. On a personal level, men like Jack were toxic to her. After getting to know him, she'd filed him in the well-to-do womanizing wastrel category. But after seeing his volatile reaction to his father, it was harder to keep him there. The little he'd said revealed that Jack had probably inherited his father's fondness for women as well as the charm to reel them in.

And here she was sharing a suite with the man. He had the master bedroom with a living room in between, but suddenly it was too close.

Damn it. She should have told him what he could do with his Christmas in London.

An unexpected knock on her door made her jump. She walked over and opened it. "What?"

"I've taken the liberty of ordering dinner." He indicated the dining table behind him set with linen, china, candles, flowers and two plates.

That was all very lovely, as was Jack. He'd slipped into something more comfortable, too— jeans that fit his toned body as if they'd been made for him. As they probably had. The navy pullover sweater made his eyes look very blue especially with traces of his earlier hostility still darkening them. And it hit her like a bolt of lightning from a clear blue sky that her crush could be resurrected without him lifting a finger.

His brother had called her feisty, but she didn't feel that way at the moment. She could meet men in business and go toe to toe. She could talk capital and investments with Jack and give as good as she got. But something had shifted for her tonight and she wasn't entirely sure what it was or how it happened. She just knew the sight of him produced a tickle low in her belly and she was aware of him in a way that she shouldn't be.

"I'm not very hungry. It's getting late. I'll just—"

"We're still on New York time. And after leaving the restaurant you clearly expressed your displeasure about not staying because the unbelievably scrumptious smells made your mouth water."

Not as much as now, she thought, forcing her gaze from the width of his chest. She'd seen him in sweaters before. She'd seen him in jeans. But she'd never seen him angry enough to do battle. And after battle warriors had an overabundance of adrenaline to channel into other activities. Physical, intimate activities. How inconvenient for her that she was handy, yet exciting for her at the same time, which just meant that she needed serious therapy.

"The scrumptious smells are gone. And since when do you pay attention to my whining?"

"Did I say whining?"

"No, but that's what you meant. It's a flaw. I'm working on it," she informed him.

"Speaking of work, I'm the boss. And you need to eat. I'm not a heartless slave-driver."

"And you're attempting to prove that by making sure your indentured subordinate is well nourished and has the strength to give you the last ounce of blood?" she asked, indicating the food on the table.

One of his dark eyebrows lifted. "When did you develop a flair for the dramatic?"

"I've always had it."

But seeing a different side of Jack had unleashed it. She knew his business background and venture-capitalist-on-the-rise story, but until today she hadn't realized how little she knew about him personally. She'd shared details of her life but he never had, unless it had been about the female of the month. The arm candy never lasted much longer than that before he ended things and it didn't affect her. Except for the occasional overly emotional cast-off who had trouble dealing with Jack's rejection and came to Maddie for consolation, in the form of an old-fashioned session of male-bashing.

But this male didn't look as if *he'd* take no for an answer. If he ever made up his mind that he wanted more from her than simply sharing a meal, she'd be in a lot of trouble. She'd never been more grateful that she wasn't his type.

"Okay, Jack. Let's eat." She picked a chair, then sat and lifted the metal covering over the plate. "Christmas dinner," she said, surveying turkey with all the trimmings.

When she started eating, Maddie found she

was hungry and the food was delicious. "Who'd have guessed hotel room service on a holiday could be so yummy?"

"In a five-star hotel one doesn't have to guess. One counts on it, which is why one stays there."

"If one can afford it." She knew Jack could afford it.

They ate in silence for a few moments, then Maddie made the mistake of looking at him. The brooding expression on his face tugged at her, because Jack didn't brood, and again she was amazed by how little she knew him. On the one hand she was safer not learning anything new. On the other, that damn dark expression on his face made her want to do something to make it go away.

"So can we talk about your family?" she asked.

"No."

She dragged her fork through the mashed potatoes so the dammed up gravy could escape.

Glancing at Jack, she realized he looked like a
man with dammed-up feelings in need of
release. And that was why *she* couldn't take no
for an answer. "I thought you were going to
deck your dad."

His gaze narrowed on her. "Did you now?"

She noted that he'd elevated the non-answer to
an art form. "You never told me you had parents."

"Everyone does. It seemed that confirming
the obvious was an insult to your intelligence."

His smile held no humor and made her shiver.
But that didn't stop her. "I guess your parents
are divorced? So where's your mother?"

"Dublin." He cut a piece of turkey and
forked it into his mouth, his gaze not leaving
hers as he chewed.

"Are you going to see her?"

"I suspect I'll have occasion to visit."

She took a hearty drink of the wine he'd
poured. "I meant while we're here."

"Technically this isn't Ireland. London is in England."

"Thanks for the geography lesson." She knew he was deliberately trying to sidetrack her. She knew he could chew her up and spit her out if the focus he turned on her got personal. But she'd developed a tough façade so that he didn't walk all over her and was never more grateful than right now. "Just so you know, the British accents were a big clue for me. To put a finer point on it, I meant since we're so close, are you going to visit?"

"There's a time issue. I'm not sure—"

"For God's sake, Jack, we came all this way. To pop over to Ireland is like going from New York to New Jersey."

"I'll think about it."

Maddie studied the dark look. Jack acted on instinct, gut feeling, deciding yes or no in a split second. He didn't think about it. That was her job. She knew he'd already made up his mind and decided to change the subject. For now.

"I liked Emma." She finished the wine in her glass and he refilled it. "She seems nice."

"I don't want to talk about my family."

As if she needed it, there was another red flag that something wasn't right with him. He was normally open and honest, too honest. On a regular basis he told her more than she wanted to know about his current woman. But now he was closed off and detached. What was up with that?

And the way he was looking at her... Maddie had shared dinner with him before, but not like this. They'd ordered in at work, and on the intimate scale it had never even registered. But this was *intimate*. God knew she wasn't experienced, but she'd have to be a moron not to feel the pent up sexual energy in him. And all that energy directed at her seemed to be affecting her brain function, which no man had managed to do since college. She had to deflect it somehow.

"Tell me about Max?"

Something flared hot in his eyes, burning through the shadows. "What about him?"

"Well, for one thing, he's very cute."

"Looks can be deceiving."

"Speaking of looks," she said, "there's a family resemblance. Does he treat women like tissues, too?"

"Tissues?"

"Disposable—like tissues."

"Max isn't your type," he said again.

"How do you know what my type is?"

"I've met one or two. The accountant." He sipped his wine as he thought for a moment. "The computer geek. The chemistry professor. There was no chemistry. With any of them."

"Like they're going to show chemistry in front of my boss."

"If the spark is there, one can't hide it."

"A lot you know." She was hiding her feelings from Jack right now she thought, as he focused those amazing eyes on her. Her pulse stuttered and she took a deep breath. "Going from one woman to the next doesn't exactly satisfy the prerequisites for advanced chemistry."

He leaned back in the chair and twirled his wineglass. "Just think of me as a scientist—experimenting until I get it right."

"Don't even go there with me. You wouldn't know chemistry if a science experiment blew up in your face. And it does on an annoyingly regular basis."

"And you know this how?"

"Two words. Angelica Tedesco."

"Ah. A lovely girl." He rested his elbows on the table and smiled his big-bad-wolf smile.

"Girl being the operative word." She shook

her head. "I had to pick up the pieces when she came to the office in tears."

"While it lasted, the relationship was mutually satisfying."

"It never lasts, Jack. Why is that?" She folded her arms on the table.

He lifted one broad shoulder dismissively. "I'm not looking for anything permanent. Don't I get points for sending roses and breaking it off before someone gets hurt?"

"You're a hit-and-run player. How do you know there's no such thing as love at first sight?"

A dark eyebrow arched. "Maddie, I had no idea you were such a romantic."

She ignored the way his words pricked her. "You may not get hurt, but how do you know others don't?"

Maddie hurt for all the Angelica Tedescos in his life. And roses wouldn't mend a broken heart. She knew for a fact only time would do that. Time and a promise not to make the same mistake. Jack had mistake written all over him.

She met his gaze. "It occurs to me that you're a lot like your father."

"You're wrong." His voice was sharp enough to cut glass.

"Am I? What was it you said to him tonight? Buried in work and playing with women? You described yourself, Jack."

His gaze jumped to hers as the muscle in his jaw flexed. "Aren't you just full of questions and observations."

"It's part of my job and what you expect from me," she shot back. "And here's an observation for you. In spite of that, he seems like a charming man."

He scowled. "Believe me, he's not the nice man you think, Maddie."

She waited and hoped he'd say more, but he'd shut down tighter than an airport in a blizzard.

If he expected them not to talk about what happened tonight, he'd brought the wrong woman to London.

"Jack, we all have flaws. Yours is a reckless streak that makes you very good at what you do."

"Your point?"

She stopped and waited until he looked at her. "Your father is no doubt imperfect, but he loves you."

The dark look got darker still and his blue eyes glittered with something dangerous. "And you got that from an observation?"

"No. I got it when he told you it's been a long time."

"I'm not following," he said, shaking his head.

"That meant he's missed you."

"Oh, really?" He leaned forward.

"Yes, really. And when he said you've done well, that meant he's proud of you."

"I had no idea you were gifted in reading between the lines."

"It's easy to read between the lines when one isn't emotionally involved," she told him. She set her fork down on her empty plate.

"And you think I am?"

"Oh, please." She rolled her eyes. "He's your father. You love him and he loves you."

"And you know this—how?"

"When you abruptly announced it was time to go, he tried to get you to change your mind."

"Translation?"

"I love you. I've missed you. I'm not ready for you to leave so soon."

He laughed, but the sound was bitter and harsh and completely humorless. "Not that I buy into such a lunatic theory," he said, "but how do you know this?"

"My father." She pushed her plate aside. "He used to tell me I looked like a college football quarterback and I found that fairly offensive as I prided myself on being feminine."

"And doing a fine job."

There was that gleam in his eyes again as he let his gaze boldly roam over her. Along with the compliment, it produced a warm glow in the wasteland of her heart. She wished she could blame the feeling on the wine, but that simply explained the buzz. This sensation was so much more. It was all that attention zeroed in on her. It was exciting. It was scary. It was a stepping-stone to heartbreak.

"I complained to my mother and she explained it was approval. That he was actually saying that I'm trim and fit."

"I couldn't agree more." Jack's gaze lowered for a fraction of a second.

His attention was more than scary. It made her want to run but she wouldn't because she'd be humiliated and Jack would win. She forced herself not to look away. "That's when I started translating male speak," she explained.

"Fascinating."

"I'm convinced your father was trying to reach out—"

"I don't want to talk about it." He stood abruptly. "Did you leave room for pie? I had it made specially. Let's have it in the sitting area." He took one of the pieces on a dessert plate and walked over to the sofa.

And just like that the conversation was over. "All right."

She took the other piece of pie and followed him. The suite, ironically enough, was decorated in the color of money. Thick jade carpet cushioned her bare feet and furniture covered in varying shades of green was arranged in a conversation area on one wall. Maddie sat on the sofa at a right angle to him and concentrated on eating her dessert.

"This is really delicious. Almost as good as my sister Susie's. The whipped cream is to die for," she said, closing her eyes. Memories of a past holiday flitted through her mind and she started to laugh.

"What?" Jack set his untouched pie on the table, then rested his arm on the end of the sofa.

"I was just remembering the time my mother caught us squirting the whipped cream straight from the can into our mouths."

"A hanging offense if I ever heard one." This teasing man was more like the New York Jack.

Relaxing, she set her plate with half the pie uneaten beside his, then curled up on the love seat. "It's funny now, but my mother was not amused." She rested her chin in her palm as she looked at him. "Do you remember what your favorite Christmas present was?"

He grinned. "A bike. Top of the line. I'd been lusting after it for months. Cut a picture out of a catalogue and hung it in my room. What about you?"

"A doll house. With furniture." She sighed. "It was—"

"What?"

"You'll think it's silly."

"No, I won't," he vowed. "Give me a chance to screw up before you make me guilty."

"You've got a point," she agreed. "Okay. It was that tweener time—"

"Excuse me?"

"That time between when you believe in Santa Claus and when you suspect the truth. I wanted to believe, but I'd heard the ugly rumors."

"Gossip does spread."

"I was like you and the bike, wanting that doll house so badly it was all I could think about. But I knew my parents couldn't afford much that year. My sister got braces. We needed a new car. Money was tight." And why was she spilling her guts? It wasn't what she and Jack did. But she'd started this. "Anyway, I decided to go see Santa with my younger brother, Dan."

"Dan was a believer?"

"Yeah. But he was intimidated by the beard and suit. I sat on Santa's lap to coax him into it. Mom wanted a picture."

"And you told Santa what you wanted?" he guessed.

"On the off chance that he was magic, I sort of whispered it in his ear." She shrugged and self-consciously toyed with a strand of hair. "Pretty silly, huh?"

"On the contrary—" He reached over and put his hand on hers.

The touch was warm, strong, sweet, and stopped her heart. It could have been the wine, the buzz, or sharing a suite with Jack, but the feel of his hand on hers was like a punch to the gut and it took two deep breaths to get everything moving again.

That had never happened before.

"Did you get it?"

"What?" she asked.

"The doll house?"

"Oh. No. Anyway—" she eased her hand from beneath his "—tell me about your bike."

"It was blue. And it didn't come from Santa," he teased.

"I knew you thought I was being silly. It's very sad when you have to grow up."

"It is, yes." He looked at her, an odd expression on his face. "If you still believed, what would you ask Santa for this year?"

"Florence," she said.

"Who?"

"Not who," she said, laughing. "Italy. I've always wanted to go there." She shrugged. "I'm not sure why. I've seen pictures, but I just have a feeling it's one of those places you have to see with your own eyes."

"Who knows? Maybe Santa will make it happen."

"Maybe."

When he smiled, the scary exciting feeling came back with a one/two punch. It was time to call it a night before she said something else she'd regret.

"I'm exhausted. Funny how sitting for hours on a plane can do that. I think the traveling has caught up with me."

Amusement disappeared from his eyes, replaced by what looked like regret. "I'm sorry, Maddie. I shouldn't have made you travel on Christmas. You had plans. With someone special?"

"Yes." Not quite a lie; her friends were special. "But it's okay. Actually, this turned out to be a nice holiday after all."

The brooding look was back, as if he were remembering the ghosts of Christmas past. Quite frankly she'd never seen a man more in need of a hug.

He stood and held out his hand. When she took it, he tugged her to her feet and into his arms. They were pressed together from chest to knee and it felt really good. If he hadn't looked so lonely, she might have been able to resist but she couldn't help herself. She put her arms around his neck and held him close.

"No matter what you think," she said, "your family was happy to see you."

"I'll take your word for that."

She looked up and his eyes flared with something hot as his gaze settled on her mouth. Was he going to kiss her?

She held her breath, suddenly wanting to feel his lips on hers more than she'd ever wanted anything—including that doll house. But she didn't dare toy with Jack.

He looked at her for a long moment, before lowering his head to settle his mouth on hers. One soft touch and her breathing went from zero to ragged in a heartbeat. He tightened his arms around her, fitting her body more closely to his, setting off sparks inside her. The needy moan trapped in her throat threatened to make her go up in flames. This was a place she'd never been before and didn't want to ever leave.

But this was Jack. Her boss.

She would never know how she managed to find the willpower and presence of mind to pull her mouth from his and disentangle herself from his arms. "It's time to turn in."

That breathless, needy voice couldn't really be hers, could it?

He ran his fingers through his hair. "Merry Christmas, Maddie."

"Same to you, Jack."

She hurried into her room and shut the door, heart pounding as if the devil were after her. The devil in the form of Jack Valentine? She'd certainly seen his dark side, a side she hadn't known he had. A side she'd have been better off never finding out he had because she was drawn to it. The dark side was what made her hug him. And that led to…

She leaned against the door and pressed her fingers to her still-tingling lips. If only it hadn't been a good kiss. But it was without a doubt the best kiss she'd ever had.

Now she hoped there wouldn't be the devil to pay.

CHAPTER THREE

ALL Maddie had wanted was a dreamless sleep and to wake up and have the old Jack back. She hadn't seen him yet, and she could say the same thing for sleep thanks to that kiss. After two years, why now? And what did it mean? Probably nothing. By sheer numbers, the women in his life proved that. Maddie wanted more. Jack teased her about the men she dated, but she'd never hear the end of it if he found out she was a virgin.

Her current state of purity had everything to do with crappy judgment in men. She'd fallen head over heels once, with a bad boy of course. She'd almost given him what she'd been saving for marriage but had found out just in time that he'd bet his buddies he could get her into bed. He'd lost the bet.

So now her taste in men leaned toward the ones who showed no obvious signs of bad boy-itis—no earrings, tattoos or long hair. The problem was she didn't want to sleep with any of them either. Up until last night, Jack hadn't tempted her but she couldn't let a nothing kiss change anything because he didn't want a per-manent relationship.

She looked in the full-length mirror on the closet door to check her appearance, then gathered up her notes on the dresser beside Jack's gift. She'd forgotten to give it to him yes-terday so she grabbed it, too. The door separ-ating her room from the shared living space was in front of her and she tried to tell herself that this was no different from going to the office in Manhattan every day.

But herself didn't buy the lie because she knocked once. She never knocked when she entered her office. "Ready or not, here I come."

"I'm ready." Jack was sitting on the sofa where he'd been last night. His laptop was on the coffee table and in the dining room there was an array of food ranging from scrambled eggs and bacon to pastries, croissants and fruit.

"This is very nice of you, Jack," she said, looking at the spread.

"I'm a nice man."

Like his father. But he wouldn't want to hear that and he was looking like the old Jack. No need to bring out the dangerous side of him that thrilled the part of her susceptible to his type.

She set her notes and his gift down on the coffee table and helped herself to eggs, a croissant and fruit, as well as a cup of coffee. Moving back to the sitting area, she took the same space she'd occupied the night before and settled the plate in her lap and the coffee on the table.

She picked up the gift and held it out. "Here. This was in my suitcase. I didn't get a chance to give it to you last night."

He hesitated to take it. "Maddie, I— You shouldn't have."

"Why? We exchange gifts." She took a bite of croissant, then a forkful of eggs.

"That's just it. I—"

"You left my visa gift card in New York?"

"Well, yes," he admitted. "I don't have anything for you to open."

"It's all right. You brought me to London."

"Under protest."

"About that," she said.

"What?" His gaze narrowed suspiciously.

"I may have slightly exaggerated my plans with that someone special."

One dark eyebrow lifted questioningly. "And yet you were still annoyed."

"Besides the whining, how do you figure?"

He held up the plain-wrapped package. "No dangling candy canes. Or snowmen. No cute little santas or reindeer." He shook it gently as he studied the wrapping. "And the paper isn't shiny."

Yet another Jack Valentine revealed. He noticed and remembered how she wrapped Christmas packages. That was endearing and she'd never figured him for the endearing type. It was information that wouldn't help to snuff out her emerging and disturbing feelings. But he *had* apologized for spoiling her plans so the least she could do was be gracious.

"I was annoyed at your timing, Jack. And the fact that you think you can say jump and I'll ask how high. But I'm over it now. I sincerely mean that. Now open your present."

He ripped off the paper and nudged up the lid

on the box, then lifted out the eight and a half by eleven butter-soft leather portfolio with his initials embossed in the bottom right corner. His gaze jumped to hers. "This is beautiful, Maddie."

"And it's personalized so you can't take it back," she pointed out. She finished her fruit.

"I wouldn't dream of it." He looked sheepish and darned if it wasn't charming. "This makes me feel even worse about not giving you a gift. I'll make it up to you."

"Not necessary. You promised me London."

"Thank you for this," he said, then set it on the table beside the laptop. "So, let's get to work. Old business first."

"Okay." She set her empty plate aside, then took a sip of lukewarm coffee before handing him the file on a software company they'd been nurturing. "They just signed a deal for shelf space in one of the country's largest office supply stores."

He scanned the notes, then looked through the spreadsheet. "Excellent. The internet sales are good, too."

"Yes. The company is performing better than we expected."

"I see that." He looked through every file. The results were all positive.

"Good work, Maddie." He put the folders on the table. "What else have you got?"

"We had twenty proposals submitted and I whittled them down to five for market evaluation. I have the top three for you to look at."

He took the first file she handed him and read carefully. "Mothers of Invention."

"I'd like to start a company to market the creations of problem-solving mothers."

His gaze captured her own but she couldn't read the expression in his eyes. "Mothers who *solve* problems?"

"You sound surprised by the concept."

He just shrugged in reply. The brooding look was now back and Maddie decided not to ask any further questions. If anything, it was silly to be disappointed that he didn't elaborate. Knowing more had made her hug him. And he'd kissed her. It would be better not to know more. She needed to concentrate on business and forget the dangerous man she'd glimpsed last night.

She cleared her throat. "As you'll see in my notes, the items range from videos that entertain toddlers, a gizmo that prevents said unentertained toddlers from unrolling a toilet-paper roll, to the obsessive compulsive mother who created a washable fabric cover for a grocery cart."

"These are problems?"

"For the average mom," she clarified.

"What about the ones who aren't average?" he said, still inspecting her report. But the muscle in his jaw contracted.

Did he mean above or below average? His frown made her wonder again what he was thinking. Something about his own mother? And again she reminded herself this was business, not personal. Up till now they'd concentrated heavily in the technological market and this was an area they hadn't tapped into yet. Diversification was good—in business. There was a lot of wisdom in not putting all your eggs into one basket. In love? She didn't want diversification and Jack was a master on the subject.

"Rather than investing in a single item," she said, "it occurred to me that one company with a line of unusual items to address the nagging chores and concerns of motherhood would be fresh and original."

"I agree," he said. "Pull it all together."

"Okay." She made notes to herself before handing over another file. "Here's one I thought would appeal to your inner technological geek."

"Cell phone central," he said, nodding as he looked it over.

"It adds even more functions to a device most people are already carrying. I've had it analyzed by our expert gadget guy and he says it looks promising."

Jack nodded and made notes in the new portfolio she'd given him for Christmas. "Whatever you think."

That was what she'd figured he'd say. Nine times out of ten he approved her ideas, and it pleased her. She handed over a file with the last of her recommendations. This was another area where Valentine Ventures had yet to venture. She'd met with the young entrepreneur and his enthusiasm was contagious. She'd assured him that Jack's go-ahead was in the bag.

"This is a restaurant proposal—"

"No." He frowned again.

Jack Valentine wasn't a serial frowner. Twice

in one meeting never happened. How could she not want to know more if he kept doing that? First mothers, now restaurants had touched a nerve with him. Although she couldn't see the connection, and it made her want to know more.

"I'm aware that restaurants are uncertain, but look at the location. It's midtown New York, yet the rent is really reasonable and the concept young and fresh. With backing it could be the next hot spot for Manhattan singles looking to hook up."

He shook his head. "I don't want anything to do with a restaurant."

"Why?"

That muscle in his jaw jerked again. "I don't know anything about it."

His tone caught her attention. She'd only heard that particular edge to his voice one other time— yesterday when he'd confronted his father. "You don't know anything about guards for the toilet-paper roll either. That's my job. I believe in this one, Jack. Very strongly." She sat up straighter. "And I'll go to the mat on it. I all but promised this guy."

"That's not like you." He took her measure for a long moment. "I guess you'll have to find a way to un-promise."

They'd worked together for two years. It was fun and she liked helping him decide what to spend his millions on. She'd gotten used to Jack taking her advice and she was surprised bordering on offended that he'd arbitrarily said no. But this was more than ego. Her gut was telling her his negative on this particular proposal was deeply personal.

"It's not like you to turn me down without a good reason. Care to enlighten me?"

"Not really. No."

"Then I don't understand," she said, unwilling to take his no without a challenge. "This project has the potential to be big, to franchise in Chicago and Los Angeles. It could catch on with serial daters not unlike yourself—"

That was uncalled for; she had no right to judge. Except she'd never seen him as he'd been at the restaurant last night and she couldn't help wondering if he had his reasons. But finding out Jack wasn't as shallow as she gave him credit for had its own risks.

"I'm sorry, Jack."

"Forget it. What we have here is a stalemate." One corner of his mouth curved up. "It's my experience that the best way to handle an impasse is with delicate diplomacy."

"Define delicate," she said.

"Let's table this proposal until we get back to New York."

"Okay. Fair enough."

"We're leaving this evening."

Her gaze snapped to his. "What about the business you had here in London?"

"We have a meeting later today," he said vaguely. "Then we're going home.

"You promised me a couple days here."

"I'm sorry. I have to get back."

"So apparently I should take lessons from you about un-promising."

"I have business waiting."

"Fine. I understand."

Who was she kidding? She didn't understand anything. This wasn't like the fearless, reckless Jack she knew. This wasn't the confident bad boy who oozed charm. This same man she'd relegated to the bad-boy section had come to London to meet his sister's new husband and now was just as anxious to leave. What was he running from?

He lifted his gaze to hers and there was confusion with a generous dose of wariness in his eyes. "As easy as that?"

"You're the boss." She gathered up her notes and started out of the room. "I'll be back in time for the meeting."

"Where are you going?"

She glanced over her shoulder because she didn't want to miss his reaction. "To lunch at Bella Lucia."

Jack sat in the town car with Maddie beside him. He'd much rather have lunched with her at the hotel. Last night's intimate meal had been something of a surprise. He always enjoyed bantering with her, but there'd been something different—intimate—something about sharing memories had pulled them closer. She'd hugged him, for God's sake, then he'd kissed her. In that moment he'd *wanted* her. But it was *Maddie*.

They were the same two people. They'd worked together over two years. In all that time, he could have put the moves on her, but he'd been careful not to cross that line and change the good working relationship they had. Five minutes with his father had brought out something in him that had moved her to hug him. He didn't want to risk a repeat of that kiss which was why he'd rather lunch with her anywhere but Bella Lucia.

"It probably isn't open today," he said.

"Why wouldn't it be?"

"Government buildings and small businesses are closed." At least one could hope. After being in New York all this time, he hadn't thought about the holiday. "It's Boxing Day."

Maddie stopped staring out the car window and looked over her shoulder at him. "As in fisticuffs? As in no hitting below the belt and go to your corner Boxing Day?"

"No. As in boxes of food, clothing and gifts that are distributed to the less fortunate."

"I thought that was done at Christmas," she said.

"It is. This is an extension of the holiday and keeps the spirit of giving alive one more day. So, there's a good possibility the restaurant may not be open."

The car pulled up to the curb in front of Bella Lucia just as four people were walking out the door with leftover containers in their hands.

Maddie looked at him. "Either it's not closed. Or those people are some of the less fortunate who just got lucky."

Jack refused to comment as he escorted her inside the restaurant where they were seated at a cozy table for two.

He didn't want to be here, but he didn't want Maddie here by herself.

"This is nice." Maddie's voice interrupted the bad memories that were threatening and he looked up from the menu he'd been pretending to peruse.

"It's all right."

So far today he hadn't seen a single member of the family, which suited him just fine. There was always the chance of a Valentine sighting, but he hoped to avoid it.

The restaurant was busy, crowded. And he and Maddie were tucked away in a quiet corner. The white table linens were perfect, as were the flowers and red tapers in crystal holders. It had five-star ambience, although he hadn't tasted the food yet. If it passed muster, he'd be damn curious to know why the business was in financial trouble. Impatient, he tapped his fingers on the pristine tablecloth, then looked at his watch.

Just then a waiter appeared with a basket of linen-wrapped bread that he set down on the table. "Good afternoon, sir, madam. Are you ready to order?"

After the waiter had taken their orders and left, Maddie broke off a piece of Italian bread and steam escaped as she dropped it on her plate. "Something bothering you, Jack?"

"Of course not."

He didn't miss the expression on her face that said she was waiting for him to explain what had happened last night. He knew she was curious; he knew all of her expressions. Including the new one that had told him she'd wanted him to kiss her last night. That's why he was cutting short the trip. He'd paid his debt to his sister and soon he and Maddie would be on their way back to New York.

"Mmm," Maddie said, taking a bite of the bread. She closed her eyes and her curious expression changed to one of sheer pleasure.

The look was positively erotic and heat shot straight through him. An image flashed through his mind of him, Maddie, tangled legs and twisted sheets and he couldn't begin to explain why now. Why the scent of her was suddenly so…vivid. Sexy. That was just one more reason why he was impatient to get the hell out of here. What was supposed to be a quick trip to clear his conscience had turned complicated. Seeing Emma and Max had generated feelings that were complicated. Now feelings for Maddie had turned complicated.

Jack hated complicated.

And that didn't sweeten his temper. "Actually, there is something bothering me."

"Oh? Fire away." She wiped crumbs from her full lips with the linen napkin and waited expectantly.

"I take exception to the serial-dater crack," he said, trying to take his gaze from her mouth.

"Okay," she said slowly, her tone implying she was humoring him. "I believe we talked about this. Sometimes the filter between my brain and my mouth isn't as efficient as it should be. Another flaw I'm working on. It won't happen again."

"Yes, it will. Because you can't help yourself."

"I promise to try."

"If you say so."

He didn't really want her to hold back, but it was a mixed blessing. Mixed because she'd voiced her observations, but she didn't know his father as he did. Mixed because he'd seen the disappointment in her eyes when she'd asked why he treated women the way he did. For reasons he couldn't explain, he didn't like that Maddie was disappointed in him.

Her gaze moved away from his and followed a slim figure moving toward the exit. "Isn't that your sister?" Before he could respond, she called out, "Emma?"

Where was that filter when he really needed

it? Jack thought as his sister turned, looked, then came toward them.

"Hello, you two." Emma smiled at Maddie, but the look she gave him was guarded.

"What are you doing here?" Maddie asked.

"I just came in to see some old friends. They wanted to hear all about how the Meridian monarchy commissioned my services for Sebastian's coronation, which is how we met."

"Very romantic," Maddie said.

"Very," Jack echoed, wryly. These two had bonded over tiaras and he could only wonder what might be next. But his sister must be very good at what she did to have snagged such a high-profile assignment. Nagging guilt twisted. He was a powerful man who could make or break a career, yet he didn't know as much as a brother should about his own sister's career. The thought tweaked his temper.

"So where is the king?" he asked.

"He's waiting for me at our hotel."

"Don't let us keep you," he said.

"Jack." Maddie looked surprised before glaring at him. "Have a seat, Emma," she invited, indicating the chair to her left.

Emma sat. "I'm going to miss working with Max." She sighed.

Maddie looked puzzled. "Is Max a chef too?"

"He's manager at Bella Lucia Chelsea, along with my father. He—Max, that is—advised me to live my own life and not worry about things here, but I feel badly adding another headache for him to deal with, he's such a workaholic as it is."

Jack knew she was simply sharing information with Maddie the way women did. Like tiaras. But he felt the words scratch at something buried deep inside and he didn't want to go there. "His work ethic must please your father."

"He's your father, too," Emma shot back. "And Max takes the business very seriously."

"So the family owns this restaurant?" Maddie asked.

"Jack didn't tell you?" Emma glanced at him. "There's three in all, Bella Lucia Chelsea is the flagship property."

"I see." When she looked at him, Maddie's gaze held censure mixed with a dose of hurt. As if he'd kicked a kitten. He disliked the look.

"What's this about a time of need?" she asked.

Hesitating, Emma looked at Maddie, then him. Jack knew his sister was being discreet in front of non-family, but there was no one more trust-worthy than Maddie. He could have blown it off, but he wanted to know what had caused the flourishing business he remembered to flounder.

"What's wrong, Emma?"

She nodded, recognizing he was giving her the okay to discuss it. "There's a serious cash-flow problem. To make a long story short, money was embezzled and the business is nearly bankrupt. Without an infusion of capital it won't survive."

"That definitely qualifies as a time of need," Maddie said. "What are you going to do?"

"The question is what Jack's going to do," Emma countered. "I didn't want to bring up anything unpleasant last night, but we have to talk about it."

"I'm going back to New York tonight," he said.

Emma's mouth pulled tight. "So you don't care that a business begun from our grandfather's love for his bride, and nurtured with the blood, sweat and tears of two more generations of Valentines, will cease to exist?"

"In a word? No."

Emma shook her head. "The Jack I remember wasn't so unfeeling and he was deeply committed to proving he had a future in this business."

"You could have said all this on the phone, Emma."

"I could, yes. But I wanted you to have to look me in the eye."

Anger churned through him. "So that crap about wanting me to meet your new husband was nothing more than manipulation?"

"Call it what you want."

"That's what it is. This family doesn't need me to bail them out. They've got the Queen of Meridia."

Emma's gaze turned steely. "There are so many things wrong with that statement, I don't even know where to begin. Suffice it to say that Sebastian is family by marriage, but you're family by blood. Who has more responsibility?"

"Are we talking about the same family that turned its back on me twelve years ago?"

"You left. I think there's some gray area in terms of who turned away from whom," she said tightly.

"It's black and white for me. I'm just

supposed to forget about the past and hand over money."

"Not forget," Emma said softly. "Learn from it, then take the high ground. There's more at stake than money, Jack. It's about mending fences with family."

Jack had never thought of himself as vindictive, but it was a heady feeling to know that he held his father's fate in his hands. He could almost taste revenge and wondered how sweet it would be. The thing was, all he had to do was nothing.

Emma's glare intensified as the silence dragged on. "You're impossible, Jack, so much like Dad it's really quite amazing."

"And you're still trying to please him," he ground out, deliberately not looking at Maddie.

"For goodness' sake, Jack, don't be such an idiot."

The friction between him and his sister was almost a tangible thing and Jack had nearly forgotten Maddie was there until she applauded. They both stared at her.

"Do you know how many times I've wanted to say that to him?" Maddie wasn't the least bit intimidated by his glare.

Emma smiled but there was a stubborn glint in her eyes. "Have at him, Maddie, with my compliments."

Maddie met his gaze across the elegant table. "Your lordship, you're being a complete idiot."

"That said—" Emma stood "—I have to run. Sebastian and I will be here a while longer if you change your mind and want to talk." She looked at Maddie. "It's been a real pleasure meeting you. I hope I'll see you again soon."

"Count on it."

"Excellent."

Emma turned away, but Jack was staring at Maddie, wondering about her comment.

"I've never known you to say something you don't mean," he said.

"I don't."

"Well, how can you see my sister soon if we're leaving?"

"It's quite simple, Jack."

The stubborn expression on her face gave him a bad feeling there was going to be a problem and he'd been told that millionaires had them.

Maddie met his gaze. "You promised me time in London and I intend to have it. I'm not leaving."

CHAPTER FOUR

JACK hadn't said much after she'd made her announcement, but Maddie knew he'd been thinking about it. All through their afternoon meeting he'd been giving off tension like radiation from a leaky nuclear reactor. On the way back to the hotel, he kept glancing at her and frowning. They'd just returned to the suite and Maddie slipped out of her cashmere coat. After setting it on the back of the love seat, she faced Jack, who was studying her intently. The look was dark, dangerous and her heart responded with a quick, automatic stutter before settling into normal rhythm again.

"So, the meeting went well, don't you think? A technology company is right up your alley, but tech toys for kids is a new area for you. I bet you liked that new shift tricycle design."

"Back wheels that move closer together as it picks up speed is a pretty innovative way of incorporating training wheels." He folded his arms over his chest and leaned a hip against the arm of the love seat.

The gaze he settled on her sizzled with something unsafe and she couldn't help thinking about that kiss. The memory of all that heat warmed her deep inside, a frozen place she'd abandoned.

She moved around him and sat on the love seat. "I was amazed at the advancement of dollhouse technology. And what I thought was an especially brilliant touch was hooking two houses together and one teenage girl calls the other."

"Things do happen when women talk."

Maddie had no doubt that was a not-so-subtle

reference to her and his sister. And probably her own announcement that she was staying. Waiting for him to say what he thought about it was driving her crazy. "I was thinking that this technology company might integrate well with Mothers of Invention," she said.

"It seems like a good risk."

She met his gaze. "As opposed to a restaurant venture?"

His mouth pulled tight before he said, "Just tell me what's on your mind, Maddie."

The more important question was what was on his. "I'd like to talk about your family being in restaurants and how that relates to the fact that you refused to put capital into a promising restaurant venture because you don't know anything about the business."

"I don't. Not any more."

"Not since your family turned its back on you twelve years ago?" she asked.

He straightened away from the sofa and started pacing. "Do you remember everything I say?"

"Yes." For over two years she'd learned nothing about him and now seemed to soak up every tidbit of information like a super-absorbent paper towel. "So you were, what—" she did the quick math calculations "—eighteen when you got out of the restaurant business?"

He stopped in front of her and looked down. "I left home and went to New York."

"That's some teenage rebellion."

"My father and I don't get along."

"I noticed. But it must have been a heck of a fight to make you leave home." She watched him carefully, trying to read into his tight expression. "What happened?"

"It was so long ago I don't even remember."

The flash of anger in his eyes told her he was

lying. But she decided not to push. She might not know facts and details about Jack's past, but it didn't take psychic ability to realize his past and family tensions were responsible for bringing out the dark side of him. But easy-going or enigmatic, she didn't think his stubborn streak would change. When he made up his mind about something she'd learned it was pointless to scale his position head-on. She'd find a roundabout way to get in.

"Okay." She nodded. "If you don't want to talk about that, can you at least tell me about your grandfather and the love story that started the family business?"

He shrugged. "William Valentine was sent to Naples as part of a British campaign in World War II. He met Lucia Fornari and married her in nineteen forty-three."

When he stopped, she wanted to shake him. How like a man to leave out details. "And?"

"When they returned to Britain, he opened a restaurant in Chelsea in honor of his new wife and called it Bella Lucia."

"Beautiful Lucy," Maddie whispered. She met his gaze and waited expectantly. "And?"

"Eventually he opened two more locations. One in Knightsbridge, the other in Mayfair." At her exasperated look he added, "Apparently William managed the business until he died in June."

Maddie processed the information and was taken aback. "So you haven't seen your family in all this time?"

He shifted uncomfortably and rested his hands on his hips. "Before you start, keep in mind that I was busy surviving. Not having a dime to your name makes it tough to keep in touch."

He'd had nothing, had been only eighteen and in New York on his own. Oh, Jack, she thought. Why did you put yourself through that when you had a family who loves you? But all she said was, "What happened?"

"I survived." He shrugged. "Eventually I received a small inheritance from an uncle on my mother's side and I turned that into Valentine Ventures."

"Okay." Maddie could understand being busy. "But after your business was successful what excuse did you give yourself for not seeing Emma?"

"She was working on her own career as a chef for Bella Lucia."

"So what made you come back now?"

"Do I need a reason?"

"After twelve years? I think so," she said. "I can see it on your face. Looks a lot like guilt."

Jack shifted and in anyone else it would be called squirming. But the mighty Jack Valentine didn't squirm. "Okay. Our parents split up and I took off. Emma was left to deal with the whole mess. She asked and I owed her." He shrugged as if that explained everything. When she simply stared at him he frowned. "What?"

Maddie folded her arms over her chest. "So you don't get along with your father."

Jack looked at her as if she had two heads. "You heard what I said. He neglected his family and was unfaithful to my mother with his many women."

"Many women? And yet you think you're nothing like him." The thought of Jack's women touched a nerve in that frozen place inside her. She wanted to keep herself numb and feel nothing, because the way she'd responded to his kiss told her the potential for pain was there in a big way. "The only difference is that you never married one of *your* many women. Why is that?"

His gaze narrowed on her. "Because I like women."

"That's not an answer."

"Let's just say I have more to offer as a friend and lover than a husband." When she opened her mouth to ask more, he held up a hand. "Enough said."

Common sense and self-preservation were sending the same message. She couldn't afford to let the attraction he'd stirred up boil over. That would be bad because he was industriously avoiding marriage and she wouldn't settle for less. In college she'd been used as a bet. She'd tried again and learned the guy was using her to get to Jack for project capital. She wanted a man to love her and commit to her. She hadn't yet given herself to a man because she wanted it to really *mean* something.

She nodded. "Okay. But probably you should be heading to Heathrow."

"Because?"

"You're going back to New York today."

He looked down at her. "You're determined to stay?"

"Yes. I have vacation time coming and I'd like to see some of London."

"By yourself?"

"Yes." And she simply couldn't resist tweaking him. "Or maybe Max would consider showing me around."

"Any tour my older brother would give, you wouldn't want to take." His voice was nearly a growl as he bit out the words.

"You haven't seen him in a dozen years, Jack. How would you know this?"

"Because when I was here, Max was the older brother every guy wanted. He knew how to party and took me to the best of them. He introduced me to fast women and faster cars."

His reaction didn't disappoint her, but it did make her curious. He'd never shown the slightest bit of emotion before when discussing her dates. What was different? Was it London? Or was it family tensions that brought out this side of Jack? This side was one she liked too much.

"It sounds like Max would know where to take me. Don't you worry. I'll be fine. You have a good flight back." She stood and started to go back to her room. "I'll check out of the hotel after I find a place to stay."

He stopped her with a hand on her arm. "Don't bother."

"No bother. I'm sure I can get a room—"

"I'll stay."

"Are you sure? Business is waiting."

"We'll work here."

"Good." She smiled sweetly. There was just one more shove she wanted to give him. "Then you'll have plenty of time to call your ultra cool older brother and he can get you up to speed on all the latest techniques with fast women."

"We caught up last night."

"Oh, please. I can't believe you wouldn't want to see him and reminisce about those women." She lifted an eyebrow.

"Not really."

"Here's the thing, Jack. Either you get in touch with Max. Or I will."

"Why are you being so stubborn about this?"

"Just because." Because she felt the conflict in him and sensed he didn't know what to do about it. "And I'm serious."

He stared at her for several moments, taking her measure. Then he nodded grimly. "All right. I'll call Max."

Jack was glad his brother had suggested they meet at a non-Valentine restaurant. Definitely neutral territory. Near Grosvenor Square, the restaurant Max had suggested was an elegant location oozing art-deco ambience—from its three-tiered light shades to the delicately etched glass panels in the windows.

With Maddie between them, he and Max were seated in a quiet corner. As he studied his brother across the table that damn empty feeling twisted inside him again when he wondered where all the years had gone and what he'd missed.

Max had ordered and approved a bottle of Alsace Pinot Blanc. He lifted his half-full wineglass. "To reunions."

"Reunions. Preferably not high school." A musical tinkle sounded when Maddie touched glasses with each of them. "So, Max, unless I miss my guess you were flirting with me the other night. And I have to ask—is there a Mrs Max?"

"No."

Jack wished there were, especially when he noticed his brother's gaze lower to the neckline of Maddie's black chiffon dress. If only it were up to her neck instead of low enough to reveal a tempting hint of cleavage. This was not a good place—torn between pleasure at seeing his brother again and a tightening knot in his gut that could be jealousy.

He wasn't sure why he felt the need to keep her away from Max, but thought it might have something to do with seeing a glimpse of that little girl who loved doll houses and believed in Santa. But he was well aware that Maddie was all grown up now. He'd given in to temptation and kissed her, a kiss that never should have happened.

Maddie had accused him of being like his father, and she hadn't meant it in a good way. The truth was, Robert Valentine had sired Max, too, and Jack didn't know his brother any more. He had no idea if his brother was a womanizer like their father. But he wouldn't let Maddie be hurt—not by Max or himself.

"I can't believe there's not a special woman

in your life, Max." Jack wondered at his brother's frown.

"Believe it."

Maddie sipped her wine, then said, "Jack told me you taught him everything he knows about women."

"Did he now?" A gleam stole into Max's eyes. "Did he happen to mention the line he used to meet women?"

"No." Maddie's blue eyes were bright with curiosity. "What was it?"

Jack groaned. "We don't really need to talk about that."

"If I remember correctly," Max said, ignoring him, "it was, 'Haven't I seen you somewhere?' Followed two beats later by 'Oh, yes. You were in my dreams.'"

"No!" The look she settled on him was both appalled and amused. "Tell me he's making that up."

"I wish I could," Jack said ruefully, but the memory made him laugh. The times with his brother stood out bright and happy in a past that was littered with darkness and pain.

"Did it work?" she asked.

"Brilliantly," Max answered. "He made me so proud."

Maddie shook her head. "I'm deeply ashamed of my gender, to fall for a line like that."

"The line had nothing to do with it," Max said. "It was the legendary Valentine charisma."

"Oh, please," she protested. "Jack was eighteen. And teenage girls are notoriously vulnerable."

Jack didn't like to think about a vulnerable Maddie fending off men. No one knew better than he how single-minded a man could be when he wanted a woman. "Is that experience talking?" he asked her.

"I like to think I was smarter than the

average teenage girl." Maddie smiled, but it didn't reach her eyes.

Jack leaned back and rested his arm along the top of the leather booth, very near her smooth-as-silk shoulder. He struggled to keep his mind on the conversation and off imagining what the bare flesh under her black chiffon was like. "Max tutored me, but there was some skill involved. I had to pull out all the stops to compete with him."

"I'm seven years older," Max scoffed. "It was no contest."

"For you." The words were out before Jack thought and he hoped no one picked up on it.

Maddie took her linen napkin and settled it in her lap. "So you felt competition?"

He should have known she'd zero in on the slip since not much got by her. Still, it had been a long time ago. He had nothing to lose by admitting the truth. "Yes, I felt it."

Max frowned. "I wish I'd known. The truth is that the age difference made it an uneven playing field." He turned a grin on Maddie. "And that wasn't his only disadvantage. I got all the Valentine charm and I'd be delighted to give you an opportunity to judge that for yourself."

"Back off, Max." Jack was consumed by another unreasonable flash of jealousy mixed with a healthy portion of protectiveness. "Maddie's working. She doesn't have time for—"

"A personal life?" she interrupted. "Maybe it's time I made an exception."

"Not with Max," he snapped.

"Apparently you haven't outgrown your competitive streak." Max lifted one dark eyebrow. "Just so the rules of engagement are clear, are we rivals over women in general? Your assistant in particular? Or does the competition include anything else?"

"Not any more," Jack snapped, refusing to discuss Maddie.

"Meaning?" Max asked.

"Nothing. It's not important."

Maddie stared at him. "If it's not important, what's the harm in telling him?"

Jack knew the issue would have more importance than it deserved if he didn't answer. He met Max's gaze. "I always felt as if I was competing with you for Dad's attention and respect."

"If that's the case," Max said evenly, "fate has given you the perfect opportunity to get the upper hand."

Jack glared at his brother. "Here comes the pitch for money."

"Emma told you about the financial problems we're having," Max guessed.

"She did." Jack noted the steely look in his brother's eyes. "If I got involved, I'd expect controlling interest. Taking the business apart and selling it in pieces holds some appeal."

"How can you even consider that? You're a Valentine," Max snapped.

"By birth, yes." Jack tensed. "But in practice I haven't been one for a long time."

Max scowled. "It's more than business. It's a heritage."

"Not from my perspective."

"So you're turning your back." Max's mouth pulled tight. "I should have expected that."

"Meaning what?" Jack demanded.

"It's what you do best. You wanted Dad's respect but all you managed to get was his attention—and not in a good way. Screwing up a big event at the restaurant, then taking off to parts unknown, is irresponsible. Me, Emma, the rest of the family—" Max shook his head. "We didn't know for a long time if you were dead or alive. You wanted respect?

Selfish, self-centered behavior isn't the way to get it."

Jack curled his hands into fists. "You have no idea what happened."

"Enlighten me."

For a moment, Jack recalled what his mother had done, what he himself had done to keep the truth from his father. He could still see the furious contempt on Robert Valentine's face when he'd said Jack wouldn't amount to anything. That he couldn't stand the sight of him. That he was his mother's son because no son of his could be so incompetent.

"Forget it." Jack felt the rage surge through him—red and righteous and consuming. He started to rise, then felt Maddie's hand on his.

"Jack, put yourself in your brother's place. How would you have felt if Emma had disappeared without a word? Or Max? Or someone else you cared about?"

He looked into her blue eyes, filled with concern and compassion. The softness and warmth of her fingers seared through him and touched that cold, empty place that never seemed to fill up. Her words, her cool logic slowly penetrated and cooled his anger.

Something unfamiliar pulled tight in his chest as he thought about her disappearing from his life. He relied on her in business. He respected and admired her. On top of that she was a beautiful woman. But this…attraction…wasn't about business. And if it wasn't about business, he wouldn't let it be anything. He was a risk-taker, but he wouldn't risk losing her.

Jack flexed his fingers, forcing himself to relax. "Okay, Max. You have a point. I left without a word."

"Did you just admit you were wrong?" she asked, one slender eyebrow lifting.

He met her gaze and grinned. "No."

Max laughed, lightening the mood. "Another Valentine characteristic, I'm afraid."

"A blessing and a curse," Maddie commented.

Max smiled at her, then met his gaze. "Seriously, Jack. The business was profitable once. The cash flow problem is simply the result of money being misappropriated. Dad is a brilliant businessman."

"I never said he wasn't."

"They say you're a lot like him."

"I've heard that, too." And he was sick and tired of hearing it.

"You need to go see him," Max continued. "Obviously you didn't get where you are by being stupid and it would be stupid to let emotion influence your good judgment. Bella Lucia is a good investment. Trust me."

Jack nodded. "I'll give it some thought."

He saw the look in Maddie's eyes and knew "it" was going to get more than thought.

CHAPTER FIVE

BACK in the suite and comfortable in velour pants and matching cardigan jacket, Maddie cradled a snifter of brandy in her hands. It was cold outside and she was grateful for the liquid fire that warmed her clear down inside. She'd been warmed in a different way when Jack had instructed the driver to take them on a tour of London at night, which was probably the best time to see any city. Darkness and strategically placed lights hid flaws and highlighted perfection. Kind of like Jack. He was the kind of man whose perfect looks turned heads, but she was finding out his life was anything but perfect.

She was sitting on the sofa with her feet tucked beneath her watching him pace back and forth in front of the windows. "So you'll think about seeing your father?"

"I said I would."

"Have you made up your mind already, or is there really something to think about?" she persisted.

"Always."

"Is that why you're pacing like a man in charge of quality control in carpet durability?"

He stopped mid-pace, then walked over and sat beside her. The sofa cushion dipped from his weight and his nearness seemed to suck all the oxygen out of the air. She wondered why she'd never noticed that at the office in New York, or if oxygen deprivation was a fact of life after kissing Jack. If so, that would make it difficult to continue doing the job she loved.

"Pacing helps me get rid of excess energy," he said.

She tapped her fingernail against the side of her glass and a crystal tinkling sounded. "Hmm."

"What does that mean?" he asked sharply.

She shrugged. "Just a noncommittal response to let you know I'm listening. It's supposed to encourage you to continue talking."

"I don't want to talk."

"How do you feel about listening, then?"

"Depends on what you have to say."

"For starters, that pickup line from Jack Valentine the early years really stinks."

The grin he flashed warmed her faster than the brandy. It was the same grin from the same man she'd known for over two years but, like oxygen deprivation, after kissing him the potency factor had increased exponentially.

He rubbed his eyebrow. "Do you want to talk about being a vulnerable teenage girl?"

"Not even for money."

"Okay, then, let's agree to put the past to rest."

"Not so fast. I do want to talk about Max's suggestion that you see your father."

"I had a hunch you would." Jack leaned back and settled his arm across the back of the sofa. The casual pose was at odds with the dark, restless, reckless look in his eyes.

"The thing is, Jack, you have to go."

"Actually, I don't."

Maddie figured this wasn't much different from taking sides when they had a difference of opinion about business. She decided to approach it the same way.

"Then tell me why you're so opposed to seeing your father after coming all this way."

"Besides the fact that we had a falling-out?"

"That was twelve years ago. Don't you think it's time to get past it?"

"What if I don't want to?"

"Why wouldn't you?" she asked.

"I already told you."

She tapped her lip. "You said he was unfaithful to your mother with many women and a workaholic who ignored his family," she said. "That's in addition to the falling-out for which I have no specific details." She sipped from her glass and felt the burn in her throat. "Care to tell me what happened?"

Jack abandoned the casual pose and stood. "Just drop it, Maddie."

"No." She swallowed the last of her brandy, then set the snifter on the coffee-table.

"I'm ordering you to lay off the subject of me and my father."

She stood and crossed her arms over her chest as their gazes locked. "No."

His mouth pulled tight as something flared in his eyes. "Disobeying a direct order is insubordination."

"If this was about work, I'd agree. But it's not."

"Exactly. It's not business. So why are you getting involved?" The edge in his voice was sharp enough to cut glass.

"You involved me when you insisted I come along on this trip."

And Maddie wished she'd been smart enough to say no then. Everything she'd thought she knew about Jack was changing. He was far more complicated than she'd given him credit for and that was frustrating and fascinating in equal parts. Frustration with Jack wasn't new, but she didn't want to be fascinated by him. He was too much like the guy who'd hurt and humiliated her.

She could overlook her attraction to Jack when she painted him with the same brush as the jerk who'd pretended to care for her. But because she'd come along on this trip, she was learning things about Jack. He had a past filled with secrets. He was pushing away the family reaching out to him. The more she learned, the more determined she was to help him reach back.

Jack stared at her. "I wanted you here because I had business and I rely on your advice."

She chose to ignore the "business" qualifier. Whether he wanted to or not, he was going to listen to what she thought he should do with his family.

"Here's my advice," she said. "Invest in Bella Lucia. You'll get more than money in return."

"I don't want more than that."

"Money doesn't keep you warm at night," she blurted out, regretting her phrasing almost instantly. Jack was never at a loss for a woman to warm his bed, and that bothered her.

"That's true, but it buys lots of blankets."

"It's family," she protested. She thought about what he'd said to Max, but Jack had always been about building a business, not tearing it apart.

"How can you even think about breaking up the restaurants and selling them off in pieces?"

"Because in this case the pieces are worth more than the whole."

"You can't look at this from a professional level. It's obviously personal. You might make more money, but it could cost your soul."

"My father cut out my soul twelve years ago. If I buy it back, it will be on my terms."

Jack's eyes glittered dangerously and Maddie shivered. "You need to talk to your father."

Two people alone in a room were like a blank computer screen. If you sat in front of it long enough, there was a good chance you'd put something on it. If Jack and his father were forced to face each other, they would talk about the past and iron out their differences.

"What if I don't want to?" Jack asked.

For just an instant she got a flash of the stubborn little boy he must have been.

Charming and strong-willed, he had probably given his parents fits. He was still charming and strong-willed and giving her fits. One had to be strong to handle him. If one wanted to handle him, which Maddie most definitely did not.

"If you refuse to listen to my advice, I plan to involve myself incessantly until you do talk to him," she warned.

He shot her an obstinate glare, took her measure and apparently decided she wasn't bluffing because finally he nodded. "Have I ever told you how annoying I find you?"

"The feeling is mutual."

Maddie hoped a meeting would put things right because she found herself between a rock and a hard place. She didn't like loose ends and couldn't go until Jack made some attempt at peace with his family. But if she didn't return to New York soon, finding him annoying would be the least of her problems.

That kiss could become a big problem if they were here too much longer. She wasn't sure she could resist if he turned into a stubborn man who wanted her.

Jack looked at his father's large white stucco town house in South Kensington. Leaving the bad memories behind hadn't been easy and he wasn't looking forward to the reminders he knew were inside. But he'd seen Emma, Max and shown Maddie some of London. He'd get this face-to-face over with then take his stubborn assistant back to New York so they could both be home for New Year's Eve.

Maddie pressed the bell, then glanced at him. "This might be easier if you didn't look as if you're going to your own execution by firing squad."

Her wry expression and trademark tartness almost made Jack smile. He trusted her, in spite of the fact that she was the one who'd insisted he call his father.

The door opened and a slim, petite brunette stood there. Her green eyes assessed them seconds before a friendly smile brightened her face. "You're early. If you're Jack."

"I am, yes. And you are?"

"Melissa Fox. I guess we're sort of related since my mother married your father."

Maddie quickly stuck out her hand. "Maddie Ford. Jack and I work together."

"A pleasure." Melissa shook her hand. "Mum and Robert are expecting you. Please come in."

She stood back and they entered a wide foyer just off the living room. At that moment a buxom blonde in an emerald-green lounging outfit descended the stairs with a small white dog in her arms. The woman's hair fell just past her shoulders and was stick-straight.

She crossed the foyer and held out her hand. "I'm Beverley. And you must be Jack. You look a lot like your father."

No need to ask if that was good or bad. He already knew the answer. "Hello."

"Mother, this is Maddie," Melissa said.

"It's nice to meet you both." She held up the dog. "And this is Saffy."

Jack refused to shake the dog's paw. He had limits, ones even Maddie couldn't prevail over.

Melissa grabbed the coat slung over the banister. "I'm glad you're early so I had a chance to meet you."

"You won't be joining us for dinner, Melissa?" her mother asked, stroking the dog.

"Sorry. I've got plans." She shrugged. "I hope we'll see more of you, Jack," she said, opening the front door.

Not if he could help it.

Beverley frowned at the door her daughter

had just closed, then turned a smile on them. "Why don't we have drinks in the living room?"

"I just want a few minutes with my father."

Her smile faltered but she recovered quickly. "Robert is probably in his game room."

Jack remembered it. "I know the way."

"We'll join you," Beverley said.

"Why don't we let the men talk?" Maddie brushed a hand over the dog's head. "I'd love for you to show me around, Beverley."

The other woman looked doubtful. "Are you sure?"

"Absolutely," Maddie confirmed.

Jack agreed because he didn't want Maddie to witness another unpleasant scene and didn't doubt that was what would happen. It was his father after all.

Jack stepped into the living room and it was like a walk down memory lane. The Bohemian rugs scattered over the carpet had belonged to wife number one—Georgina. Diana—wife number two—had been into American kitchens. The O'Briens' Irish coat of arms hung on the wall—a memento of wife number three: Cathy. His mother.

Before the grinding resentment took hold, he noticed the life-sized ceramic tiger, panther and giraffe. Since he didn't remember them, they must reflect the questionable taste of wife number four. Dominating the room was a glass coffee-table resting on four gold elephants and he couldn't quite suppress a shiver as he moved through the room. No wonder his father was happiest in the game room.

And no wonder Jack was alone. He'd grown up in a house that was like a museum to bad relationships. It didn't take a PhD in psychology to understand that he always broke things off with a woman before anyone's heart was seriously damaged. With Jack it was all about wining and dining and fun. Then he was gone before he could destroy a woman the way his father had his mother. He wouldn't put a woman through that.

Winding his way through the house, Jack followed the faint smell of chlorine to the indoor pool. The air was humid and the windows fogged with moisture where they met the cold outside. Robert was sitting in a lounge chair by the pool—with a glass of whiskey beside him and a cigar in his fingers. He was dressed in slacks and a pullover sweater with the white collar of his dress shirt sticking up at the neckline. When the older man saw him, he smiled.

"Hello, son." He stood. "You're early. Why don't we go into the living room and have drinks before dinner—?"

"No." Jack ignored his father's outstretched hand.

Robert looked momentarily surprised, but

nodded. "All right. I can get you something from the bar." He indicated the game room, separated from the pool by French doors.

"Don't make this into a social occasion."

His father frowned. "What's more social than a son coming home?"

The anger knotting inside him was familiar and welcome. "Since when am I your son? As I recall, you wanted nothing to do with me because no son of yours could be so incompetent."

"That was a long time ago."

"I screwed up," Jack said bluntly. He was itching for a fight. He could feel it clawing through him.

"You were young. I said some harsh things. You said some harsh things." He shrugged.

"Yeah." Jack still remembered calling his father a son of a bitch and it hadn't made him feel any better.

"That wasn't the first time we had words. But

there was something different that night. What was it, Jack?"

He'd covered for his mother because there had been no one else to protect her, but he was surprised his self-absorbed father had noticed anything out of the ordinary.

"The difference was that I realized nothing between us would ever change."

"Why did you disappear, Jack?"

"Why didn't anyone look for me?" he countered.

"I hired a private detective," Robert said.

That stunned him, but he hid the reaction. "Oh?"

"He located you and confirmed that you were in good health."

Jack found that hard to believe. "Right."

"The man reported back to me that he'd tracked you down where you were living in a despicable little room in New York. You were working as a busboy in a restaurant that I can't remember the name of. Quite a comedown, my boy."

Jack remembered the room—rats and bugs and yellowed walls. He'd cooked on a hot plate or survived on peanut-butter sandwiches. Or brought food from Gimme Sum—the Chinese restaurant where he'd worked. When he'd had no money, he'd learned where meals were served at a rescue mission. And every moment had been consumed with proving his father wrong, proving that he would be a success.

"I'm not your boy. And I was never contacted by a detective."

Robert tamped out his cigar in the ashtray on the wicker table beside his lounge chair. "His orders were simply to find out where you were. Clearly you wanted your space. You knew where the family was. If you needed help, you only had to ask."

Jack curled his hands into fists as anger

swelled. Come crawling back? No way. "Is that your segue into asking for money to bail out your failing business?"

Something flashed in Robert's eyes. "If it were *mine* it wouldn't be failing. My brother got us into this fix. John covered for his son the embezzler."

That confirmed what Max had said. "So it's all Uncle John's fault for helping his son?"

Robert's mouth pulled tight. "If your uncle had the same connection and commitment to the business that I do, he'd have found another way. My father started that restaurant for *my* mother, not his. John always resented that."

Ironic, Jack realized, that he and Max had different mothers yet had maintained a warm relationship in spite of their competition and desire to please their father.

Robert set his whiskey on the glass-topped table beside the ashtray. Cigar smoke still hovered over it. "Just think, Jack. If you invest the needed capital it will give us an edge. We can run the company. Father and son."

"Ease Uncle John out?" Jack asked, struggling to keep his voice bland. "What about Max? And Emma?"

"She's the Queen of Meridia now. I think her days as a chef are behind her. And Max wants what's best for the business."

That was probably true about Emma. But the Max Jack remembered wouldn't like the idea of squeezing out a family member who'd worked his whole life in the business.

"What do you say, Jack?"

"Would you really trust me with controlling interest?"

Robert's gaze narrowed. "Why shouldn't I?"

"Because I could take it apart and destroy you."

"Is that what you're planning?"

"What would you do in my place?" Jack demanded.

His father had the reputation of being a brilliant businessman and Jack had been told he was like him. His father was a cold-hearted bastard who would screw anyone—even family—for the sake of the business. Was Jack like that, too?

"Never mind. I don't want to know." Jack saw the surprise that flashed in his father's eyes, then turned away and left the room. He found Maddie where he'd left her in the foyer with Beverley.

"Jack?" Maddie's blue eyes filled with concern when she looked at his face.

"We're leaving," he said curtly.

"But—"

"Now." He was in no mood for more of her advice. Taking her arm, he led her to the door.

"Nice to meet you, Beverley," she said over her shoulder as he hustled her outside. "Give Robert my regards."

When they were back inside the town car, she turned on him. "That was rude."

"Quite."

"What happened with your father?"

"He said with my money and his brains we could rule the world as father and son."

"Don't be sarcastic," she said. "Tell me what really happened."

"I told him what I would do with controlling interest in the business."

"But, Jack, you don't mean—"

He held up a hand to stop her. "I'm not in the mood for you to defend him. Have I ever told you how obnoxious I find this glass-is-half-full attitude of yours? Why can't you just hate him like I do? Just on general principle?"

"That's just silly." She shook her head. "I don't even know him. And neither do you. Not any more."

She was right about that, Jack thought. And he didn't want to get to know Robert

Valentine. He was afraid he'd find out more to hate about himself.

In spite of what he'd said, most of the time he liked Maddie's attitude. It balanced him. Balanced him right into this disastrous meeting with his father. He couldn't think of anyone besides Maddie who could have talked him into coming here. At least it had taken his mind off kissing her. Ever since that kiss, he'd felt his attraction growing stronger.

It was time to get back on familiar ground. Now that he'd seen his father, they could go home. They could resume their comfortable working relationship and life would be good again.

After instructing the driver to take them back to Durley House, Jack looked at Maddie. "I'm going to have the company plane ready in the morning to take us back to New York."

"But—"

He held up his hand. "I'm ready to go."

"Not so fast, your lordship. There's something I forgot to tell you."

He had a bad feeling he wasn't going to like it. "What?"

"Emma called earlier. She invited us to a New Year's Eve party at the Meridian Embassy in London. I accepted on your behalf."

"You'll just have to un-accept."

"But I really want to go. I've never been to an embassy, let alone a party there. You should know that I'm prepared to go by myself, even if it looks weird to not have a date. Before you answer, give it some thought."

He hated that he couldn't flat out say no because he recognized in her the essence of the little girl who'd once believed in magic. "All right. I'll think about it."

CHAPTER SIX

"JACK, this has been the best day." Maddie sighed and leaned back against the cushy leather of the town-car seat.

"So you're not sorry we played hooky from work and went sightseeing?"

Not sorry. Surprised. Apparently he'd gotten over being angry at her for talking him into seeing his father.

"Sorry? Oh, please. This is me."

"I know," he said, a *faux* serious expression on his face. "I was afraid you'd implode when I suggested breaking the rules and taking a day off."

"I'm organized, not inflexible."

Her heart stuttered and skipped when she glanced sideways at him. He looked so good. That dark hair, mussed as if he'd carelessly run his fingers through it, yet so perfect for him. Blue eyes that danced when he laughed, brooded when he didn't. In jeans and navy sweater, he looked every inch the wealthy bad boy. Staying in London had put them in contact 24/7 which was probably why she was beginning to overdose on his appeal. She'd enthusiastically embraced the opportunity to leave the seductive confines of their suite.

"Let's just say I appreciate your dedication," he said. "And I think it should be rewarded."

"Well, there's nothing like a trip to Buckingham Palace to let a girl know she's appreciated."

He rested one arm along the back of the leather seat. "You do realize you're not the first person to try and get a rise out of the guards?"

"You mean the guys in the funny hats and bright red jackets?"

"They're very well trained."

"They'd have to be," she scoffed. "In the states, any guy who went out in public dressed like that had better be able to defend himself. Or run like the wind."

Jack laughed. "Actually I meant they're trained not to show emotion, or give any indication what they're thinking."

Just like you, she thought. Maybe he had been a palace guard in a past life, because she rarely knew what he was thinking. He'd put her off about the embassy party and she wondered if this whirlwind day was her consolation prize because going solo to the ball would make her look like a loser.

"Well, it was a lot of fun, Jack. Thanks for taking me."

"You're welcome."

The car slowed and pulled smoothly to the curb. Maddie looked outside at the fashionable row of shops. "Why are we stopping here?"

"An errand."

The driver opened the door and the cold air made her shiver as Jack got out. He reached a hand back to her, then wrapped his fingers around hers and tugged her into Stella's, an upscale dress shop. The inside was brightly lit by crystal chandeliers. In the center of the room was a carpeted dais surrounded on three sides by paneled mirrors. Around the perimeter, fancy dresses in vibrant colors and different materials hung on racks.

A twenty-something brunette in a sweater and skirt with a flirty, flared hem smiled. "Mr Valentine?"

"Yes. And this is Maddie."

Maddie gave him a wry look even as a twinge

of annoyance tightened inside her. Until now it had been such a perfect day.

"I'm Rhona. We spoke on the phone and I've picked out some lovely dresses for you to choose from. Size four, I believe you said?"

Dresses? Choose? Maddie pulled her hand from his. "You don't need me for this."

"Actually, I do," he said. "As you'll be the one wearing the dress to the party tomorrow night, the fit could be important. And since I'll be your escort, the public at large will have to look elsewhere for proof of your weirdness."

Her eyes widened as his words sank in. "You're going to the party?"

"With you. Yes."

Inside her, happiness swelled and spilled over. Maddie threw herself into his arms and hugged him. "Thank you, Jack."

He pulled her tight and she thought she heard

a soft sigh before he let her go and smiled down. "Now then, you need to try on dresses. This place comes highly recommended."

"Says who?"

"Says my sister Emma who confirmed it with my cousin Louise. So, off you go with Rhona."

Maddie followed the saleswoman down a corridor to a large mirrored dressing room containing several racks of dresses and two over-stuffed chairs with a table in between.

Rhona sighed. "I must apologize in advance, Maddie. We normally schedule fittings in order to give clients our undivided attention. But Mr Valentine was quite insistent that you need something for tomorrow night and apparently so does half of London. It is New Year's Eve. We're a bit short-staffed today, but I'll—"

Maddie held up her hand. "Don't worry about it. I'll be fine."

"Then have fun," Rhona said, indicating the dresses. "I'll be back as quickly as I can."

When she closed the door, Maddie went through all the racks and organized the dresses into priorities: the ones she loved, the ones that might be flattering, possibilities, and not in this lifetime. There was no way to eliminate by price because none of the creations had tags and were probably all outrageously expensive. She would just have to cross that bridge when she fell in love with something.

After slipping out of her jeans and sweater, she welcomed the challenge and quickly eliminated dresses that were unflattering or the color was wrong for her hair and skin. She'd just pulled on a strapless black chiffon and practically twisted herself into a pretzel trying to zip it without success. Maybe she could track Rhona down. Barefoot and holding the bodice of the dress up, Maddie opened the door and scanned the corridor. She followed it the way she'd come, hoping to find the saleswoman in the main area of the shop.

Rhona was nowhere to be seen, but Jack was there and spotted her before she could dart back. "Hi," she said, feeling self-conscious. "I—I was just looking for Rhona to—"

"Need some help?"

"No—it's just a zipper. I think it's stuck."

"I think I can handle that."

She'd just bet he'd done up a girl's zipper a time or two. This would never have happened if she'd stayed in New York, but Maddie didn't think she had a choice. There was no delicate way to tell him he made her nervous in the way of a woman who was too attracted to a man who didn't think about her that way. That kiss on Christmas was simply that—a holiday sweet nothing.

"All right, Jack."

She came out into the room and turned her back to him. It seemed there were mirrors everywhere and she was mesmerized by the sight of his tanned hands dealing with the delicate back of her dress. His fingers skimmed the bare flesh of her lower back and raised tingles of awareness. It felt as if he were touching her everywhere. His gaze met hers in the mirror and it was intense, stunningly intense, and all the more exciting because of that. Her breath caught, then speeded up as she struggled to conceal it. Not easy when the bodice of the dress was cut daringly low and the swell of her breasts clearly visible.

She tried to think of something to break the tension, but couldn't since her brain had also taken the day off. Fortunately Rhona came bustling into the room.

"Maddie, there you are." She looked harried

and blew out a breath as she critically studied the black dress. "I don't know about that one."

"I know," Jack said. His voice was deeper than usual and there was a raspy sort of quality to it.

"I agree, it certainly looks lovely on her," Rhona said, gazing at Maddie thoughtfully, "but I've got something in white that I think would suit better."

Jack's eyes grew dark and hot and sent desire dancing up and down Maddie's spine. "I don't know if my heart can handle better," he said hoarsely.

Rhona laughed. "Come with me, Maddie."

A short while later, Maddie was dressed and standing beside Jack as Rhona set the hanger of the dress on a hook. The dress, a strapless white silk creation, had fit perfectly. Now that she thought about it, how did Jack know her size? Because he'd had women in all shapes and sizes, of course. She refused to acknowledge the twinge. This was a lovely gesture. One she'd keep in perspective, though it threatened to expand. But this was Jack, after all.

Maddie took a deep breath, preparing herself for the exorbitant price of the dress she'd fallen in love with. "What's the damage, Rhona?"

"I'm taking care of it," Jack said.

The saleswoman smiled at him. "I assumed you would."

"No," Maddie said. "We're not— I mean I'm not his—" Wasn't this awkward? "I work for him."

That hadn't come out right. When heat crawled up her neck and flushed her cheeks, she didn't miss Jack's grin.

"I can't let you pay for this," Maddie protested.

Jack assumed battle stance as he folded his arms over his chest and stared her down. "Okay, we can do this the easy way or the hard way."

"What's the hard way?"

"That's where we argue for ten minutes and I pull rank and do whatever the hell I want."

"What's the easy way?" she asked.

"You graciously give in and let me buy this for you as a belated Christmas gift." One corner of his mouth curved up. "I prefer the easy way. I ruined your holiday and dragged you into all this stuff with my family. I've been an insensitive jerk. Let me make it up to you."

When Maddie glanced at Rhona, she knew the woman was half in love. Join the club, she thought. Who wouldn't fall for a man being so charmingly sweet, even after Maddie had assumed he'd stopped here to get something for one of his women. If she let him buy, did that make her one of his women? Not in this lifetime.

"All right, Jack. You win." She smiled. "And thank you."

December 31—Meridian Embassy

With her hand tucked into the bend of Jack's elbow, Maddie walked into the ballroom. The white silk she'd fallen for at first sight made her feel beautiful and she had to admit Rhona had been right about it. Jack had been rendered speechless the moment he'd seen her in it and she wasn't sure why that mattered so very much.

"I feel like Cinderella at the ball." Maddie looked up. "Pinch me, Jack, so I know I'm not dreaming."

He covered her cold hand with his own warm one. "You're not, Princess."

That was the closest Jack had ever come to an endearment and it meant a lot, especially when she knew he wasn't delirious with joy about being here. It wouldn't be wise to read too much into this, but he *had* come because she wanted to. And he'd surprised her with this dress. The thought produced a glow inside her.

"So, if I'm Cinderella, that would make you what? Prince Charming?"

"If the crown fits—"

His grin, sudden and spectacular, went straight to her head as surely as alcohol on an empty stomach. The tuxedo and the fact that he looked amazing in it certainly multiplied the intoxication factor.

"Thank you for bringing me tonight," she said.

"You're welcome."

She'd expected a teasing comeback and was both pleased and surprised when it didn't come, indicating he was on his best behavior. This was new.

"So," she said, "should we get in the receiving line?"

He didn't look happy. "Do we have to?"

"She's a queen now. I'm sure there are rules. Something you're not very good at."

And she must have a screw loose because the man who thumbed his nose at rules appealed to her in or out of a tuxedo. Jack was no prince, but she'd seen his charming and successfully resisted. It was the man he'd become in London who could really hurt her. But what was the harm in relaxing her guard just for one night? They were in public. What could happen?

"I'd like to say hello."

"The way you look tonight…" Blatant male approval was in his eyes as his gaze lowered, settling on a place in the vicinity of her cleavage "…how can I deny you anything?"

Maddie felt as if she were floating on air as he escorted her across the room and they took their places in the receiving line. Tables with candles, flowers and white linen cloths graced the perimeter of the room. Overhead chandeliers dripped golden light on a wood floor already polished to a high gleam and poinsettias adorned tables standing in front of walls painted pale blue and decorated with window-frame molding. A Christmas tree with splashes of red, golden bows and white lights dominated one corner of the reception area.

Their arms brushed as they continued to move forward and Maddie could almost see the sparks. She definitely felt the heat as Jack focused his attention on her and she wanted to be in line with him forever. But eventually they reached Emma and Sebastian, who both smiled with genuine pleasure.

"Maddie. Jack. I'm so glad you came," Emma said. She looked like a queen in a one-shoulder, full-skirted black chiffon gown.

"Nice of you to invite the peasants," Jack teased.

"Nice of the peasants to come," Sebastian said, but his eyes were warm with humor.

Emma looked at him. "Max tells me you agreed to look at his business plan for the restaurants."

"I did, yes. I'd discuss it with you, but, frankly, I'd rather get Maddie into a dark corner."

"Don't you just love his sense of humor?" Maddie said. But the idea of Jack and a dark corner held too much appeal.

"Who's joking?" He nodded at the other couple. "See you later."

He moved her off and slid his arm around her waist, drawing her closer against his side. A possessive gesture, she thought. With overtones of protectiveness. Jack didn't do protective. He also didn't do dark corners. Not with her, but she thought she'd like it. A lot. His best behavior could deal a major blow to her will-power. While Maddie and Jack stood on the sidelines, musicians took their places in a corner of the room opposite the Christmas tree and began to play a waltz.

He bowed slightly. "May I have this dance, Princess?"

"You may, your Lordship."

On the outside, Maddie pulled off cool, calm and collected, which was a miracle because her heart was going a hundred miles an hour. Somehow she managed to move gracefully into his arms even as tingles skipped over her skin. But she thought her knees would give out when he settled her snugly against him.

With her fingers on his broad shoulder and the other hand swallowed in his, Maddie tried to relax and follow his lead. This was another first—she'd never danced with Jack. Was *that* a good way to start out the new year? Not if she wanted to keep from getting hurt.

She forced herself to meet his gaze and tried

to think of something innocent to say. "So, have you made a new year's resolution?"

"I honestly haven't given it much thought." One corner of his mouth curved up. "Is there one you think I should make?"

She remembered what his sister had said on Christmas. "I just want you to be happy, Jack."

Surprise flickered in his eyes. "I expected something about not being a scoundrel."

"Your words, not mine." She liked the scoundrel because that made him resistible. She didn't want to know he could be more than that.

He touched a finger to her chin and nudged it up. "What about you? Any resolutions?"

Other than to keep her heart in one piece? "Continued success," she said.

A waiter was just passing with a tray of champagne and Jack let her go in order to grab two. He handed her a crystal flute. "Here's to many years of success working together."

"I'll drink to that," she said, touching her glass to his.

Food was served buffet fashion from silver chafing dishes and platters. The music was alternately lively and lovely. Jack was solicitous and suave as he stayed by her side and pretended he didn't notice any of the beautiful women in the room. Although they both smiled at Louise who was busy networking with the prestigious guests. Maddie had been to some of the most exciting parties in New York, but couldn't remember having a more elegant, enjoyable evening. She had a bad feeling it had nothing to do with the environment and everything to do with her escort.

Not unlike Cinderella, before she knew it midnight approached. The wait staff circulated with trays of champagne until each person had a glass for the toast. When the time came, everyone in the room counted down to midnight.

"Five, four, three, two. One," Jack said. He looked down at her. "Happy New Year, Princess."

"Same to you, Jack."

They sipped from their glasses just before he lowered his mouth to hers. It should have been a quick, chaste, traditional kiss, but the moment their lips touched something sizzled between them that had nothing to do with static electricity and everything to do with a sensual connection. He met her gaze and his own was filled with dark intensity as he cupped her cheek in his palm and kissed her again.

Maddie rested her free hand on his chest and curled her fingers into his satin lapel. The softness of his lips was exquisite and her heart pounded as excitement poured through her. When he traced her lips with his tongue, she instinctively opened to him, then heard his quick intake of breath. He took what she offered and plundered her mouth thoroughly, leaving her breathless and clinging to him, wanting more yet unsure what more there was.

Her chest rose and fell rapidly though she couldn't seem to get enough air into her lungs. When he dragged his mouth from hers and stared down, he was breathing hard. Maddie swore she saw yearning mixed with the tension in his eyes. He downed the rest of the liquid in his glass in one gulp.

"We've done our duty," he whispered, not taking his eyes from hers. "Let's get out of here."

In the car, on the way back to the hotel, Jack savored the anticipation flowing through him like wine. Maddie Ford turned him on and the realization blew him away. Her beauty was a given, but at work she'd always pulled primness around her like a force field.

But tonight... In the strapless dress that hugged her curves like a second skin, there'd been nothing prim about her. He was filled with the sight, sound and scent of her. If those were the only senses she'd engaged, he might have been able to hear his sensible side trying to warn him about rocking this particular boat. But the taste of her was still on his lips and that was his undoing.

When the door to their suite was closed and locked, Jack turned. "So, where were we?" he murmured. He reached out, and pulled her into his arms, then felt her tremble and heard a throaty little moan that turned the blood in his veins to fire. He knew women as well as he knew money and Maddie wanted him as much as he wanted her. "Now I remember," he said, just before settling his mouth on hers.

Another tremor of desire rippled through her and he felt wonder and a deep satisfaction at tapping into the unsuspected depths of her passion. Their bodies were molded together and her breasts pressed into his chest. Her hips tilted up against him in an almost instinctive movement that signaled her melting into him, a sure indication that he could make her his.

Jack continued to kiss her as he toyed with the little tab that would lower the zipper and part the back of her dress.

"Jack?"

He trailed kisses over her cheek as he slowly slid the closure down. "I like this much better than zipping it up."

"We better stop." Her voice was breathless.

He touched his tongue to a spot just beneath her ear and felt her tremble. Her body said everything he wanted to hear.

"That's enough, Jack."

It was the way she tensed, not the words, that finally penetrated his sensual haze. He straightened and met her gaze. "What?"

"We can't do this." With her palms on his chest, she exerted gentle pressure to push him away.

"Yes, we can."

"I'd be lying if I said I wasn't attracted to you." She swallowed.

"But?" He didn't like the sound of this.

"It can't happen."

"Why? We're consenting adults. I want you. You want me." With his hands at her waist, he brushed his thumbs up and down, just beneath her breasts.

"You want another conquest." The words were soft and laced with that damn primness.

"That's not fair, Maddie. Tell me I'm wrong. Tell me you didn't kiss me back."

Something shattered in her crystal-clear blue eyes and she looked ready to run. Then she said in a brittle voice, "I can't. And I'm sorry, but it was a mistake."

Jack shook his head to clear the rushing sound in his ears. "It didn't feel like a mistake. It felt honest, and pretty damn good."

"I agree. But we have a special relationship and this would spoil it."

"How?"

"I can't believe I have to explain this to you."

"Believe it," he all but growled.

She sighed. "Women are wired differently. Unlike men, we don't treat sex like a competitive sport. We don't jump in and out of bed without our feelings being engaged."

"So you don't like me?" Good God, now he sounded as if he were in high school. This wasn't at all what he'd envisioned.

"Liking you isn't the issue. I'm saying that when you move on to the next woman, and everyone in this room knows you will—"

"How do we know?"

"It's what you do, Jack. As soon as a woman

gets the least bit serious and wants more from you, you are so out of there."

As usual, she was right. But that didn't sweeten his temper or take away the ache of wanting her. "But this could be fun while it lasts."

Maddie's hands were shaking as she crossed her arms over her breasts, holding the front of her dress up. "And what happens when it's over? Think about it. There could be hurt feelings. That could lead to tension in the workplace. I like my job, Jack. And I know how it feels to be disposable. I don't need another lesson from you. Tonight's been fun. Let's just leave it at that."

Jack felt a lot of things, but fun wasn't one of them. However, the need to put his fist through a wall was on the top of his list.

"What makes you think men view sex as a competition? Who made you feel disposable?" It was a shot in the dark, but there was a bruised look in her eyes and he didn't like it.

"College." She looked down for a moment. "I was away from home for the first time and fell in love. I thought he loved me, too, and felt it was time to show him how much I cared for him. I'd made up my mind to take *the* step."

"What stopped you?"

"One of his fraternity buddies slipped up and I found out he'd made a bet that he could get me into bed. All I was to him was a wager. And the whole time we were together he was dating someone else so he was two-timing me on top of everything else." She held up her hand to stop him when he opened his mouth. "Before you say it, I did try again. A brief fling with another fidelity-challenged man. That's when I realized the type of man I'm attracted to is bad for me. He didn't just break my heart. He broke my trust."

Her mouth trembled and for just a moment she caught the corner of her bottom lip between her teeth. Emotions kaleidoscoped across her expressive face. Betrayal. Bewilderment. Disillusionment. But, most of all, a hurt that went soul deep. The primitive need for retribution slammed through Jack. He wanted to hurt the bastard who'd put that look in her eyes.

"The thing is, Jack, your track record with women proves that your relationships are all about quantity instead of quality. You send roses and think that makes it okay. But it's not okay for me."

She thought he was just like the bastard who'd put that look in her eyes? Good God. She thought so little of him? "Maddie, I—"

"What else is there to say? You made it clear that you don't want anything permanent. And I won't settle for anything less."

"You mean marriage?"

"It's not a dirty word."

"It's not a guarantee," he ground out.

"Maybe not. But I guarantee you're a bad risk. You'll never settle down with a woman you love, because you'll never love any woman. As they say, the fruit doesn't fall far from the tree."

"Meaning?"

"You're just like your father."

He'd lived his life trying to be different, struggling to overcome Robert Valentine's DNA. It seemed everyone made a point of telling him that he'd failed. He was sick and tired of hearing it, but most especially hearing it from her.

"Don't *ever* say that to me again, Maddie."

"I thought you always counted on me to tell you the truth."

"I count on you in business."

"Then we agree." Her mouth pulled tight. "Our relationship needs to stay strictly professional. That's settled, then. I'm tired, Jack. I'm going to bed."

When she turned and left the room, Jack saw her smooth, satin skin in the vee of her half-open dress. His hand ached to touch her, the rest of him ached to take her. All of the above proved he was a scoundrel.

He was no good for her; he'd only make her unhappy. As his father had done his mother. She was right to walk away from him.

But something told him he would regret letting her go for as long as he lived.

CHAPTER SEVEN

MADDIE knew Jack must never find out she'd exhausted her willpower in resisting him. They were a week into the new year, but she couldn't forget the way his kisses had made her hot all over. She'd never wanted the way Jack had made her want and the strain of not letting him know was taking a toll.

Jack had put on his charming face and never said a word about what had happened, but she could feel an invisible wall between them. Sometimes, when he didn't know she was watching, his eyes would grow dark and questioning, tortured, and she wondered what he was thinking.

He'd told her they would work in London until Max delivered his business plan. And every afternoon, Jack took her to see whatever touristy thing she wanted.

What she wanted was to get back the easy, working relationship she and Jack had once shared. What she wanted was to rewind to the moment when Jack had asked her to come with him on this trip. This time she would say no. Because he was different here.

And she was different, too. She'd kissed him back and wanted more.

Since that night she'd given it a lot of thought and realized he hadn't taken her to the embassy party to be nice. Although, buying her that gorgeous dress was definitely nice, but beside the point. The party was about reaching out to his sister—to family—and he probably didn't even realize. The differences in him had to be about his past, the part of his life he'd never discussed. Maybe if—

When the phone rang, Maddie set the untouched file she'd intended to review on the coffee-table and rose to answer it. "Hello?"

"Maddie, it's Emma."

She looked at the closed door to Jack's room. "Emma, I'll get Jack for you. He's on a conference call, but he'll—"

"Don't bother him. Since I've got you," Emma continued, "I just wanted to say that I hope you enjoyed your visit to the embassy and had a good time at the party. You and Jack disappeared so suddenly we never had a chance to say goodbye."

A flush crept into Maddie's cheeks. Etiquette had been the last thing on her mind after Jack's kiss. "It was— I've never had such a— I'll never forget it," she finally managed to say.

It was the truth. She wouldn't ever forget the breathtaking kiss. Talk about chemistry! Unfortunately it had changed everything with Jack, making it an uphill battle to salvage their former working relationship.

"Is everything all right, Maddie? Did something happen?" There was concern in Emma's voice.

Oh, yeah, she wanted to say. But then she'd have to provide details. "Not really," she lied.

"It's about Jack, isn't it?" There was a slight pause on the other end of the line before she said, "Let me put a finer point on the question. Are you in love with my brother?"

"Good heavens, no." Maddie sincerely hoped that was the truth. "Emma, I know you're trying to be nice, but Jack doesn't do commitment and that's what I want."

"Sorry. I'm prying. But," Emma added, "you should know that our—Jack's and mine—formative years were difficult. Be patient with him, Maddie. He could very possibly be worth the effort."

"He's not going to change."

"I'm sorry you feel that way." There was a pause, before Emma said, "Do me a favor, will you? Tell Jack I talked to Mum. It took me a while, but she told me what he did for her twelve years ago."

"And?"

"You'll know what to do. Goodbye, Maddie. It was a pleasure meeting you."

Before Maddie could say anything, there was a click on the other end of the line. Just then the bedroom door opened and Jack was there. His hair was mussed, as if he'd dragged his fingers through it. His sweater and jeans were charmingly casual. And her heart stuttered and bumped at the sight of him.

"Who was on the phone?" he asked.

"Your sister. She didn't want me to disturb you. She and Sebastian are going home and called to say goodbye."

"I see." He frowned. "That sounds pretty innocuous. Why do you look like the stock market just crashed?"

Maddie repeated what his sister had said and had a clear view of Jack's face. The intense expression put every nerve in her body on alert. What made *him* look as if he'd lost everything, as if he had no one? As if he were empty? Her heart squeezed painfully tight and made her want to put right whatever it was. Damn. She wanted to hug him again.

Hugging would lead her into temptation, a place she couldn't afford to go. But she had an alternative destination in mind. Emma was right. She did know what to do.

"So, is it cold in Dublin this time of year?" Maddie asked.

"Why?"

Maddie stared at his stubborn expression for several moments. His past was catching up with him. His grievances with his family were surfacing and she couldn't shake the feeling that it was at the heart of his restlessness. Maybe if he resolved his conflict—whatever it was—the two of them could go back to the perfect boss/assistant relationship they'd enjoyed. The relationship where she kept him in line and he didn't cross it and kiss her. The one where she didn't wonder if she was falling for him.

"The weather in Dublin matters very much because I need to know how to dress when we're visiting your mother, Jack."

Jack wasn't sure how Maddie managed to have her way with him, but she damn sure didn't use sex. Yet here he was in Ireland. He'd called his mother and she was expecting them.

After flying to Dublin, he'd hired a car and driver and they were heading up the long road to Cathy's place, about fifteen minutes from the city. The house was just coming into view. A patchwork of white-fenced corrals fanned out behind the barn. On the gently rolling green hills, scattered horses lazily nibbled grass. The setting was bucolic and made him uneasy.

Cathy O'Brien Valentine's family home was a modest, two-story structure nestled in the center of a shallow valley. It was a tranquil and serene setting, not at all the way Jack remembered his mother. High-strung, unstable—emotionally needy would describe her best. If, as his father had said, he was his mother's son, what did that make him?

In his earliest recollections, he could recall her making it clear she needed him—to behave. Be quiet. Listen to her or his father would make him listen. And he had behaved, and worked harder than ever before, after listening to his father tell him hell would freeze over before he would get another chance to screw up Bella Lucia. Max was right. Fate had given him the ultimate means of revenge.

Maddie sat silently beside him in the car. He glanced at her and saw the rigid set of her shoulders, the tension in the delicate line of her jaw.

"You're not nervous about this meeting? Are you?" he asked.

"No." She waved her hand dismissively, then clasped her fingers in her lap. Tightly. "Are you nervous?"

"Of course not." But he wanted it over.

After the driver stopped in front of the house Jack got out of the car and held the door for Maddie. As he waited he heard voices and laughter. A couple, side by side with their arms around each other's waists, came around the house.

His mother's blonde hair was much as he remembered—long and wavy. She was still plump in her jeans and thick, baggy olive-green sweater. But her smile made her seem younger somehow as she looked up at the tall, black-haired, blue-eyed man who grinned down at her. What love looked like…

Jack's guard went up instantly.

Cathy saw him then and glanced up at her companion who gave her what looked like an encouraging nod, followed by a supportive squeeze. The two of them stopped on the cobblestone walkway in front of Jack.

Cathy studied his face. "The last time I saw you, you were a mere boy. You're all grown up, Jack."

"Hello, Mum."

"It's wonderful to see you. You look really good. So handsome." The Irish accent was thicker in her voice. She lifted her hand, as if to reach out, then dropped it. When she looked at Maddie, a speculative gleam slipped into her light blue eyes. "Who's this, then? Your wife?"

Maddie's mouth thinned for a moment as she held out her hand. "Madison Ford. Maddie. I'm Jack's assistant."

Jack eyed the tall stranger. "Your turn."

"Aidan Foley." The deep tone was thickly accented and couldn't hide that he was Irish through and through. "Your mother and I are—"

"Good friends," she interrupted, putting her hand on his arm. "Please come in, Jack. Maddie. I'll make a pot of tea. We can catch up."

"We'd like that," Maddie said. "Right, Jack?" She nudged him in the ribs with her elbow.

"Yes. We'd like to know what you've been up to." His gaze narrowed on the other man.

They went in the house and Jack saw that it was comfortable and cozy, not flashy, not the way it had been when she'd been with his father. Photographs of him and Emma were scattered on the end tables and hung on the walls. A brightly colored afghan was slung over the back of the floral-covered sofa and reading glasses were carelessly resting over a facedown book on the coffee table.

In the kitchen, Aidan poked at the banked embers in the fireplace and coaxed it into a small blaze before adding several logs. Cathy invited them to sit at the pine table, then set about putting tea together. Her *good* friend helped in what clearly was an intimately familiar choreography, movements that showed they made tea together often.

They smiled at each other and their hands touched, bodies brushed. This was a long-term connection and the realization had unreasonable anger coursing through Jack.

The man in question watched carefully even as he stood back, folded his arms over his chest, and leaned against the counter. Cathy poured from the teapot, then set steaming mugs in front of him and Maddie.

"That'll chase away the chill," she said, smiling brightly, as if determined to ignore the awkwardness.

"Thank you." Maddie wrapped her hands around the cup.

"What's it been? Twelve years?" Jack rested his arms on the table and glanced at his mother's lover. Tension crackled in the air and Jack didn't give a damn. "So, how've you been, Mum?"

Aidan's deceptively casual manner disappeared when he moved and stood by Cathy, pulling her against him. "You're a guest, Jack. And Cathy's son. But when you speak to your mother you'll be puttin' some respect in your tone or I'll ask you to leave our home."

Jack stood and faced them both. "And I'd like to know who you are to my mother."

Aidan met his gaze without flinching. "I'm the man who loves her."

"So do I." Jack took a step forward.

Cathy put herself between them. "Aidan, why don't you take Maddie down to the stables and show her our horses while Jack and I talk?"

"I'm not leaving you with him in a mood—"

"It's all right." Cathy smiled. "This conversation is long overdue."

Aidan hesitated, then forced a smile for her. "If that's what you want, love."

Maddie stood and put a hand on his arm as she met his mother's gaze. "I think I'll stay with Jack."

Cathy took her measure, then finally nodded. "That's fine, then."

When his mother's lover was gone, Jack said, "Is he good to you?"

"Aidan?" Her smile was soft. "Very."

"Are you married?"

"He's proposed many times and I've turned down every one."

"Why?" Maddie asked softly.

Cathy gripped the top of the ladder-back chair. "The truth? I married your father because I was pregnant with you, Jack, and had to. I'm with Aidan because I love him and for no other reason."

"Maddie says marriage is a measure of commitment."

"I said," Maddie interjected, "that it's the right thing for me. I don't judge anyone else."

Cathy smiled. "She's a wise one. Aidan tells me he loves me and shows me as much in everything he does. It's all the commitment I need."

"He's younger," Jack pointed out, not sure why that was important.

"He is, yes. And he keeps me young. He respects me and my opinions. He has expectations of me that I find myself wanting to meet."

The words touched a nerve and Jack wasn't sure why. "What about your drinking?"

"Jack—"

Maddie put her hand on his arm again and the touch steadied him. But the words were already out there. He refused to feel like a bastard even though the blunt question bleached the pretty pink from Cathy's cheeks.

Her chin lifted and she met his gaze squarely. "You're confident and self-assured, Jack. You always have been. Though you can't understand, I'll tell you because you asked. I did drink too much in those days—to help me cope. I was barely twenty-one and overwhelmed by the demands of being a mother. Living in the shadow of my husband's love for another woman."

"More than one," Jack murmured.

"Yes." Her mouth compressed slightly. "But there was only one he loved. Diana."

Jack knew about her, his father's second wife.

He had half-sisters, Rachel and Rebecca, who'd been raised by their mother in the States.

"When she passed away," Cathy continued, "Robert told me that he would never love another woman the way he loved her. The day I drank too much and…did what I did…at Bella Lucia was the day I received the divorce papers. I was losing my husband and there was nothing I could do."

This wasn't the same defenseless woman who'd begged him not to let Robert know what she'd done. This woman didn't need him to protect her. She had Aidan, although Jack suspected she didn't need him either.

"You've changed." Resentment tinged his tone.

"I have, yes, hopefully for the better." Her smile was sad and apologetic.

"You told Emma what happened," Maddie said gently.

"That Jack protected me?" Cathy nodded as

she met his gaze, her own troubled. "I know you promised to keep my secret but I'll always hate myself for asking it of you. I'm your mother. I should have protected you."

"Yes."

"Jack, I don't know what happened," Maddie said, gentle censure in her voice. "And I don't need details. But your mother is trying to apologize."

"It's all right, Maddie." Cathy sighed. "He has every right to be angry. Jack paid too high a price."

Damn right, he thought. She'd lost a husband that night, but he'd lost his family. He'd lost everything.

The look in his mother's eyes pleaded for his understanding. "Your father's not a bad man, just flawed. He couldn't love me, and I don't think I was in love with him either. He didn't make me happy, anyway."

Now that she knows what happiness looks like, he thought, remembering Emma's words.

"What happened with your father and me had nothing to do with how he felt about you and Emma. He always adored his children. He especially thought the sun rose and set on you, Jack."

"He had a funny way of showing it," Jack bit out.

"I've forgiven him, son. It's time you did, too."

Maddie took his hand in both of hers and forced him to look at her. "Your mother is right, Jack. The past is eating away at your present and robbing you of a future. You need to let it go so you can move on. For your own sake."

Move on? Jack felt as if he'd been stranded on a desert island for the last twelve years and was just rescued, only to find out everyone he cared about had moved on without him. His mother was happy and at peace, yet he was angry and resentful. What kind of a son was he? What kind of man?

He looked into Maddie's trusting eyes. Beautiful Maddie. His sensible, stubborn Maddie. He was a selfish bastard for dragging her into this mess. The very least he could do was protect her from himself.

CHAPTER EIGHT

JACK had left her stranded!

Not stranded, exactly, Maddie admitted. Aidan had dropped her off at the hotel. But what was up with Jack? He had his faults, a great many, but leaving her without a word of explanation was not at all like him. And she was really uneasy.

She hurried inside and punched the up button to summon the elevator. When the doors didn't open instantly, she jabbed several more times. "Stupid lift," she muttered.

His mother had been upset and said he had every right to be angry and it was completely her fault. But when Maddie had pressed for details, Cathy had firmly told her she'd have to ask Jack.

"Darn right I'm going to ask him." She jabbed the call button again for the elevator that would take her to the suite. Assuming he hadn't left her stranded in Ireland as well as the outskirts of Dublin.

Fear knotted inside her. This wasn't just out of character for Jack, it was scary out of character. She'd seen the disapproval rippling through him for Aidan, but didn't understand what fueled it. His parents were divorced and had been for many years, which explained a lot about why Jack didn't do commitment. But anyone could see that Cathy looked happy and a ring on her finger wouldn't make a difference. So what was Jack's problem?

The elevator doors finally opened. "Thank God."

When it arrived on the top floor, Maddie

hurried down the hall to the suite. She unlocked the door, then walked inside, flipping on the light. She stopped suddenly when the shadows disappeared and she saw Jack sitting on the love seat. Had he been alone in the dark all this time?

"That was low, Jack." She dropped her coat and purse on a chair. "Why did you take off like that?"

The layout was not unlike their suite in London, with the exception of a corner fire-place. Flames crackled there now. But Jack still hadn't acknowledged her.

"Jack?" Hands on hips, she stared at him.

In front of him on the coffee table was a bottle of Irish whiskey and a tumbler half full of the stuff. It looked untouched.

"You left me, Jack."

"I had to get out of there."

"No kidding. Why?"

He picked up the whiskey glass and turned it,

studying the amber liquid as if it were the cure for a dreaded disease.

What had been unease blossomed into full-blown worry. "Jack, are you all right?"

"I don't think so."

The Jack she knew would never admit that. This more introspective man reached in and grabbed her by the heart. In seconds she was sitting beside him. She touched his forehead, testing for fever. Then she looked in his eyes and saw his wounded soul.

"What's wrong?"

"You were right about me, Maddie. I'm a despicable person."

"I never said that," she protested.

He turned his head and his gaze locked on hers with mesmerizing intensity. "You said I was like my father. It's the same thing."

She'd said that in a moment of anger, embarrassment, and self-preservation. She'd needed to push him away. This wasn't the time to point out that most likely his father had many positive qualities. "You're a good man."

"See, that's where you're wrong. My mother is happy and it ticked me off. If that isn't despicable, I need to look up the meaning of the word."

"What drove you away twelve years ago, Jack?"

He said nothing, although the look he turned on her was dark, desperate and dangerous, but she was determined.

She rested her hands in her lap. "Since we arrived on Christmas everyone has been dancing around it. Whatever 'it' is. You might as well tell me because I won't let up until you do."

He stared at her wordlessly, so long she was sure he would call her bluff. Then he set the glass of whiskey on the table without drinking.

"I badgered my father to give me some re-sponsibility at Bella Lucia. There was a big event, very high profile. A wedding, some politician's daughter." He stared straight ahead and his voice was monotone, hinting that he was barely keeping his emotions in check. "The flu was going around and restaurant staff was getting sick. Dad was desperate, but he gave me a chance to prove myself."

He stopped and she could almost see the memories playing through his mind. His mouth pulled tight and Maddie wanted to say something, encourage, but she was afraid to interrupt and break the spell.

"I was focused and in control," he continued. "The food was prepared, liquor on hand, wedding cake waiting—"

She put her hand on his arm, encouragement and support. But she didn't say anything.

"The day of the event I got to the restaurant early in the morning. To go through my game plan, make sure things were absolutely ready.

Leave nothing to chance. But chance has a way of biting you in the ass."

"What?" she asked softly.

"My mother was there. Passed out drunk. She'd lashed out at my father because of the divorce. It looked like the kitchen threw up. Food was destroyed. The cake—"

"Oh, Jack." She shook her head, pity for that eager, ambitious young man coursing through her. "But I don't understand. Why was your father angry with you? When he saw your mother and the mess—"

"He never did. I managed to get her out and clean the place up. It looked like nothing happened. And I mean nothing."

Maddie thought about it and connected the dots. "He thought the food had never been prepared in the first place."

"It was pathetically easy for him to believe the worst," Jack confirmed bitterly.

"Why didn't you tell him the truth?"

"She was so fragile. The divorce was a fresh wound." His voice was distant, as if he could still see Cathy that night. "He'd have completely destroyed her if he'd found out. I couldn't let that happen."

"What did he say?" Maddie was afraid to hear his answer, but knew he had to tell it.

"That I was incompetent. A screw-up. No good to anyone. And I'd never amount to anything."

And ever since, he'd paid with his heart and soul trying to prove the man wrong. "Oh, Jack—"

"He told me to get out and I obliged."

And he'd never been back after lying to his father with the noblest of intentions. Her heart ached for Jack, for the years of loneliness and pain he'd suffered.

"How does protecting your mother make you

despicable?" she asked softly, hoping he would see in himself what she did.

His gaze was overflowing with wry self-incrimination. "She moved on. She's forgiven my father. She's content with her significant other. Don't get me wrong." He surged to his feet and moved to the window, staring out while the muscle in his cheek flexed. "No one knows or understands the toll that living with my father took on her better than I do. But I resent her happiness."

His mother had found love and companionship while the son who'd shielded her had gone on alone. Contrary to his father's prediction, he was incredibly successful. Admiration and something far deeper grew inside her. But she couldn't deal with that right now. This was about Jack and he needed her.

Maddie rose and walked over to him. "That only makes you human, Jack."

He didn't look at her. "The irony is that I was only trying to prove to my father that I was worth something. And I failed."

"You're wrong, Jack. You protected your mother. You proved you're worth more than all of them put together."

He didn't acknowledge the comforting words. "So that's it. The whole ugly story. Aren't you sorry you asked?"

"No. Your mother should never have asked you to do what you did. But I'll say this again because it's very important. You need to forgive your father. If you don't, the ugly past will continue to have the power to hurt you."

"I don't think I can do that."

She put her hand on his arm, needing to touch him, hoping it would make him hear her—believe her. "You built a multimillion-dollar company with practically nothing. In my opinion you've amounted to something—and more. It's time you stopped working to prove your worth and work on allowing yourself to be happy."

He shrugged off her hand. "I'm tired of this." He sighed. "I'm tired, period. Good-night, Maddie."

She stared at his broad back as he abruptly walked into the master bedroom. It was said that a woman could judge the character of a man by the way he treated his mother. She was stunned by the fact that Jack Valentine, the man she'd assumed was shallow as a cookie sheet, had depths and dimensions and more charac-ter than she'd ever suspected. He'd *protected* his mother, taken the blame for her angry, vin-dictive actions, and his reward was exile.

He wasn't simply a good-looking man she was attracted to. He was the man she was falling in love with. And he'd been left alone too much. She wouldn't do it to him, too.

Before Maddie could think it to death and

talk herself out of it, she followed him. She crawled up on the bed to kneel beside him, then put her arms around him.

They sat like that for a long time before he reached up and pulled her into his lap and held her close. "I've never told anyone about that night, Maddie."

"I'm glad you told me." She rested her cheek on his shoulder.

Jack clawed his way out of sleep with the feeling that everything was wrong, starting with the fact that he wasn't alone in bed. A woman was lying half on top of him, her gently rounded breasts nuzzling his chest. He opened his eyes. A sliver of light from the living room caressed Maddie's tousled blonde hair and created a nimbus. One of her shapely jean-covered legs was carelessly thrown over his and her small hand rested on his chest. He let out a long breath, one part tension, three parts relief.

Maddie hadn't left him.

She felt sweet and so right just where she was. He tightened his arms around her and there was another breathy sigh of contentment, as if she connected with him on some elemental level and was at peace here with him.

Him. Jack Valentine, bachelor bastard.

They must have fallen asleep. He'd told her his secret, shared his dark resentment and it had been draining. God knew he'd felt as if someone had pulled the plug on his emotional power source. Yet, she hadn't turned away. In fact, she'd defended him and his actions. Maddie didn't hesitate to call him on the bad stuff he did, and there were times it annoyed the hell out of him. So annoying, in fact, that he'd wondered more than once why he'd brought her with him to London.

But her honesty made this moment all the sweeter because it made the good stuff she said about him almost believable. And he'd needed her, needed someone to talk to after seeing his mother.

He gently pressed his lips to the top of Maddie's head and breathed in the intoxicating scent that was perfume and sensuous, seductive woman.

She stirred against him, pressing her body to his, mumbling as if trying to get closer. He could almost feel the heat of her feminine center caressing him. All the blood drained from his head and pooled south of his belt. He was hard. He was ready.

He wanted her.

Her fingers flexed on his chest and she started to pull away until he covered her hand with his own to hold it in place. His heart was beating, pounding, a roaring sound in his ears.

Maddie stretched again and he could feel her

go from complete relaxation to groggy awareness. "Jack?"

"I'm here, Maddie."

She was silent for several moments, thinking.
Figuring out where she was. Remembering
what he'd told her. She nestled her cheek on his
chest. "Are you all right?"

Since he'd expected her to pull away as soon
as it sank in where she was, the question regarding his state of mind took him by surprise.

"I'm fine." Better than fine. Not alone.

He was New York's most eligible bachelor. A
ladies' man who'd had a great many women
and awakened with most of them, yet still felt
isolated. It disturbed him that he didn't feel
that way now.

"Thanks for—"

She touched a finger to his mouth, silencing
him. "Don't say it. I'm glad I was here. I hope
it helped."

In answer, he took her wrist in his hand and pressed her palm to his mouth. Her body went still, frozen in anticipation. One by one, he took her fingers into his mouth and sucked gently. When he touched the tip of his tongue to the tender, sensitive skin between her index and middle fingers, he heard her sharp intake of breath. Her chest rose and fell rapidly, a rhythm she'd probably picked up from him.

"Jack—" Her voice was a breathy whisper full of need and hunger. "Jack, please kiss me. I liked it so much when you did."

"But, I didn't think you—"

"I couldn't let on. Because— Well, it's not important now. Things are different. After—" She cupped his cheek in her hand. "Never mind. It doesn't matter. Just kiss me."

"Are you sure?" he asked, but his lips were already taking hers. He wasn't sure of anything except he couldn't seem to stop himself.

The touch was spontaneous combustion as she surged against him, sliding her fingers into his hair. It was like holding fire in his arms. The small sounds of pleasure she was making heated his blood. Desire exploded through him as he pressed her into the mattress, his body half covering hers.

When he traced her mouth with his tongue, she opened to him and he could no more stop himself from taking what she offered than he could hold back the sunrise. He plunged inside, stroking and staking his claim, invading her, imitating the act of making love. He teased the roof of her mouth and felt her squirm, rubbing her bare foot along his thigh.

As naturally as breathing, he moved his hand from her waist, up under her sweater, to settle on her abdomen.

"Oh, Jack," she said, her voice husky with passion.

"You feel good, Maddie."

The words were pathetically inadequate to describe the silky softness of her skin, the exquisite sensation of her bare flesh. He rubbed his thumb back and forth, just underneath her breast, just grazing the underside. Her pleasured whimper fueled his own excitement, feeding his need to feel her naked body against his own.

He slid his hand higher, resting his palm on her breast. Through the wisp of lace that was her bra, he felt her tighten at his touch and savored the wonder of her response to him. In the dim light, he could see her head thrown back in abandon, the slim column of her neck exposed, there for the taking.

A small smile played on her lips as she squirmed in his arms. "Oh, Jack. That feels so— Good."

"I love touching you."

Acting on pure instinct, he pulled far enough

away to grasp the bottom of her sweater, then drag it up and off. She sat up, and with a smoky glance over her shoulder let him know to unhook her bra, which he could now see was black and sexy. His hands shook slightly as he released the fasteners and the sides parted, revealing her slender back.

"Love *me,* Jack."

"No need to rush." Except he'd never heard quite that level of need in his own voice before.

Dropping his head, he kissed her neck and relished the shiver that shook her. He touched his lips to her shoulder as he reached around and took her bare breasts in the palms of his hands. The fit was perfect, the feel delicate, lovely, intense. He rubbed his thumbs over her nipples and felt them pebble at his touch. She was amazingly receptive and so immediately quick to respond.

Her responsiveness drove him crazy. But

she'd stopped him before, insisting that making love would destroy the good thing they had.

"Maddie?" He kissed her neck and smiled when she shivered. "I have to ask. Are you sure about this?"

"Very sure." Her voice was laced with desire. "It never felt right before. Doubts crept in. And I just couldn't do it."

"So there's not a doubt in your mind?" he persisted.

In answer, she tilted her head to the side, giving him the freedom to roam her neck at will. "None. I've waited for the right man and never thought you'd be the one. But this feels right. It feels perfect."

Waited? Right man? The one? His head pounded along with other body parts that urged him to ignore the words. But he couldn't. Doubts crept in, but surely he was wrong. "Have you ever done this before?"

She twisted her fingers together and hesitated a moment before answering. "No."

"You're a virgin?"

"That would be the correct term for someone who's never had sex." Her tone was sassy, but the underlying vulnerability leaked through.

She'd never been with a man.

Good God. What the hell was he doing?

Maddie was an innocent. He cared about her. God, he *was* despicable. He couldn't treat her the way he treated other women, experienced women looking for a one-night stand.

He dropped his hands as if he'd been burned and backed away. Sitting on the mattress, he rubbed both hands over his face as need and frustration warred inside him.

"Jack?" Maddie glanced over her shoulder. Her gaze was hidden in shadow but there was a tremor in her voice.

"You were right, Maddie. On New Year's Eve when you said this would spoil us."

"I was wrong. I want this. I want you." She turned to face him.

He looked at her, so proud, so beautiful, and didn't think he could stand much more. Maddie wanted love and marriage. She wanted someone who could make her happy. This was her gift to that man. It was special. *She* was special. If he took it from her, she'd hate him. And he didn't think he could stand it if Maddie hated him. If she didn't leave, he didn't think he could stop himself.

"It's been great, Maddie. Seeing London with you. The laughs. Spending money on you."

"But— The things you said— About kissing me."

"I meant everything." And more, he wanted to say. "It's been fun. You're terrific. And I don't want you to misunderstand because sex complicates everything."

The bruised look was back in her eyes. "I don't understand. Is it because I've never done this before?"

"It's because there's nothing between us, Maddie." He rolled off the bed, as far from her as he could get. He didn't trust himself near enough to touch her.

She crossed her arms over her breasts, embarrassment chasing away her passion and pleasure. He hated himself for making her look like that, for making her ashamed. But he couldn't do this. Not to Maddie.

"You need to go," he ground out. He needed her to leave before he couldn't let her go at all.

She gasped, a small cry, then scrambled off the bed and gathered up her sweater, covering herself as she rushed from the room. Destroyed.

Way to go, ace, he thought. DNA had reared its ugly head, proving he was like his father after all.

Jack ran his fingers through his hair, then

pressed his fists to his eyes, trying to block out everything, without success. He would never be able to block out the shock, surprise, and hurt he'd put on Maddie's face. But sending her away had been the right thing. And not just for her. He'd needed her today, and not in the physical sense.

Well, that was a lie, he thought. He'd needed her that way, too. Apparently he needed her in every way it was possible to need a woman. And he couldn't stand that he did. He didn't want to need anyone ever again. If there was any positive in dredging up the past, it was the reminder that he could only count on himself.

He'd sent Maddie away for her own good. She would thank him in the morning. And they could forget all about this.

CHAPTER NINE

MADDIE was numb when she closed her door and locked it. As if she needed a lock to keep Jack out. She could leave the door wide open, dance around naked and still be safe from him. How ironic was this? she thought bitterly. She'd waited to give herself to a man, and finally decided to go for it. She'd wanted Jack to be the one, and she hadn't given any thought to having a ring on her finger first. She wanted him simply because she loved him. And he'd turned her away.

Anger sneaked past the numbness and she stoked it to hold back the pain she knew was coming. She threw her black bra across the room, then yanked her sweater over her head. Putting it back on in front of him would have been too... Too humiliating. All she'd wanted was escape.

Maddie wished the earth would open and swallow her. She'd been humiliated when the man she'd loved had bet he could get her into bed. She'd been mortified when the story had spread all over her college campus. But that was nothing compared to this.

She was in love with a man who didn't want her. New York was teeming with models and actresses—some of the world's most beautiful women. They were the core of his dating pool.

"Dating my foot," she muttered. "A euphemism for sleeping with them." Her eyes burned, then filled with tears. "But he wouldn't sleep with me. Not even for money. He doesn't need it."

She didn't know from personal experience, but it was generally understood that men wanted sex pretty much all the time. And it was also a generally accepted fact that they took it wherever they could find it. Which made his rejection all the more pathetic. Jack didn't even have to look for sex. She'd been right there, in his arms, in his bed. Willing and ready. Boy, had she been ready. And he'd still turned her away.

Was she not thin enough? Not pretty enough? Too blonde? Not blonde enough? What was wrong with her? He'd kissed her and it had been good. Better than good.

She'd never been swept away, not even in college. Her choice to sleep with the jerk had been logical—a conscious decision to go to the next level. But when it had been over with him, she'd never felt this physical ache. And somehow she knew it was more than sex. It was the need to make love, to give herself only to Jack.

Unfortunately the thoughts pouring through her melted the numbness and she began to feel.

The pain knotted in her stomach and spread everywhere, until finally lodging like a rock in her chest. It pressed against her heart.

His rejection had nothing to do with her looks. It was chemistry. She felt it; he didn't. She'd probably been nothing more than a diversion. At least he'd had the decency to push her away before she'd made an even bigger fool of herself. Maddie breathed deeply, dragging air into her lungs along with the scent of Jack still clinging to her sweater.

"He can't love me. He can't love anyone—" Her voice cracked.

That was when her heart shattered and she knew the shards would prick her forever.

The next morning Maddie still wanted to fall through a hole in the earth. Probably not the best thing to think before getting on a plane. But she couldn't help it. After a night spent crying into her pillow to muffle the sobs, her eyes were tired and puffy. She no doubt looked hideous. If he rejected her now it would be understandable. But they'd ridden to the airport in stony silence and that showed no signs of changing.

It was no consolation whatsoever to realize she'd been right. He was toxic for her. If he'd turned on the charm like any self-respecting bad boy she'd have seen the dismissal coming and shut him down before he could draw first blood. But he'd done something worse than be straightforward. He'd opened up to her emotionally and that had been her undoing.

So here they were. Maddie, queen of till-death-do-us-part, was in love with Jack, king of one-night stands, in the airport waiting area. He sat in a row of chairs across from her, working on his laptop as if the information would bring about world peace or a cure for cancer.

She stole looks at him, even though each and

every glance produced a pain that went soul-deep. If only he looked tired and puffy, too. Or tortured. That would be good. But he just looked like… Like Jack. Handsome, intense, dark, hunky Jack. She wished…

Her cell phone rang and she saw him glance over. When their gazes met, his own was hooded before he looked down at his computer again.

Maddie flipped open the phone. "Hello."

"Hi, honey. It's Mom."

"Mom—" Maddie's throat closed as the familiar warmth seemed to reach out and wrap around her, chasing away the cold. How stupid would it be to lose control now, when she'd managed to hold it together from the hotel to the airport?

"Maddie? Are you there?" A worried note crept into Karen Ford's voice. "Is everything okay?"

Maddie got up and walked over to the

window looking out at the jet and the maintenance crew in overalls checking it over.

"I'm fine, Mom." But her throat closed again.

It felt like that time she was ten or eleven and had somehow gotten separated from the rest of her family at a big amusement park. For a long time, she'd wandered around alone and scared, looking for them. But she'd held it together until she'd finally spotted her mother and burst into tears. As a grown woman she realized she'd let go because it had been safe. With Jack so close, nowhere felt safe.

"What's going on?" Karen asked.

"I'm at the airport. In Dublin," she added. "We're on our way back to London."

"What are you doing in Ireland?"

"Jack came to see his mother. It's close to London."

"I'm aware," her mother said wryly. "You never said anything about his family."

"Because I didn't know anything."

She wished she didn't now. Seeing them again had changed Jack. The past had unleashed the darker man, intensifying the reckless streak that had made him successful. She'd also seen the thoughtful, protective side. Now she felt she knew the whole person, the three-dimensional man with flaws and frailties, strength and a depth of nobility she'd never suspected.

He was the man she'd been waiting for all her life and could never have.

"Maddie?"

"Sorry, Mom. Why did you call? Is everything okay there? Dad?"

"Everyone's fine. I just hadn't heard from you."

That was when Maddie realized she'd never appreciated her parents and family enough. She'd always taken their love for granted. A few weeks without talking and the woman was on the phone. Jack had left home at eighteen because his mother had been a basket case and his father a bastard and no one had bothered to go after him.

"I've been kind of busy, Mom. How was the cruise?"

"Amazing. You should have come with us."

Maddie couldn't agree more. "I'm glad you had a good time. Can't wait to see the pictures."

"When are you coming home?"

She wished she'd never left; she wished she were there now. The tears were threatening again. She heard a cell ring behind her and glanced over her shoulder to see Jack take a call, then signal that it was time to board. "I'll be home soon. I've got to go, Mom. It's really good to hear your voice."

"Same here. Can't wait to hear all about your trip and how things are with you."

No more than Maddie could wait to

unburden her heart. "I miss you so much. Bye, Mom. Love you."

"Love you, too, sweetie."

She followed Jack onto the plane then and took her seat. After landing in London, she unbuckled her seat belt and stood. Jack was retrieving a bag from the overhead bin and the sight of his broad back and flexing muscles brought a sharp, fresh wave of pain. She missed home; she missed her family. And she made up her mind about something else.

"Jack, I'm not going back to the hotel with you."

"Why not?" he asked, one eyebrow lifting.

"There's something I have to take care of."

He frowned. "Everything all right?"

No, she wanted to say. He'd completely mortified her. On top of that he'd hurt her terribly and she couldn't be around him.

"Everything's fine," she lied.

He stared at her for several moments, but his expression was unreadable. "All right. I'll see you later."

He acted as if nothing had changed between them and nothing could be further from the truth. For her everything was different.

Maddie took a deep breath, bracing herself to face Robert Valentine. Her first thought had been to stop by the house, then she'd realized Bella Lucia was probably where she'd be more likely to find the workaholic. She knocked once on the office door, and after hearing a muffled "Come in," she entered the room. Jack's father sat at his desk, staring at the computer monitor.

"Hello, Mr Valentine."

Surprise flashed across his handsome face. "Maddie. How nice to see you."

She cocked a thumb over her shoulder. "Max

was downstairs and sent me up. Am I inter-rupting?" If she was, she really didn't care.

"Not at all, my dear. Do sit down." He swiveled his chair to face her and held out a hand, indicating the chair in front of the desk.

She settled her jacket and purse on the other chair, then sat and crossed one jean-clad leg over the other. "Thank you."

"I assume Jack is downstairs?" If he was worried about Jack's intentions, it didn't show.

"No." She shook her head. "I came here alone."

"What a nice surprise." He linked his fingers and rested his hands on his desk. "You're looking lovely as ever. London agrees with you, I think."

That was baloney. She was aware that she looked as if she'd been run over by a truck. Effortless charm. Like father, like son. Maybe like the son, there was more depth in the father than anyone knew, and she was about to find out. Although the part of her that was hurting just wanted to walk away. That part wanted to be bitter and angry.

But she couldn't forget that Jack had wanted her here with him when he faced his family. Since the night they'd arrived in this restaurant, she'd been a bridge between him and them. She'd cross it one more time because she loved Jack. When you loved someone, you wanted them to find happiness. He couldn't do that until he resolved his past. She'd do this one last thing for him.

"I think London is a lovely city, but I wouldn't say it agrees with me. Or Dublin, either." Especially not Dublin. She drew in a deep breath.

"What about Dublin?" Robert asked sharply. "This isn't actually a social call."

His dark eyebrows drew together. "No?"

"Jack and I returned from Ireland just this morning. We saw his mother." She pressed her lips tightly together, then decided to just say it. "I came here, Mr Valentine, because I just learned the truth of what happened twelve years ago. It's time you knew, too."

"What are you talking about?"

When Maddie finished the sorry tale, the older man looked taken aback. "You're saying that Jack deliberately let me think he was an irresponsible slacker?"

"Jack said it was quite easy for you to think the worst of him."

"I see." Robert leaned back in his chair. He stared at the papers on his desk, but couldn't hide the shock and surprise of this revelation. As he processed the information and the ramifications the frown on his face deepened. Then the intense expression took on traces of shrewdness. "Why do you care, Maddie?"

She shouldn't, but she couldn't help it. "Who said I care?"

"I was just asking why you're involving yourself in Jack's past."

Jack had asked her that once and she'd told him it was his fault for insisting she come with him for Christmas. Now she knew it was deeper than that, but she wasn't going there with his father.

"Jack is my boss."

"Forgive me, but this seems above and beyond an assistant's duties."

She wasn't going to let him make this about her. This was about Jack and his family. She'd seen for herself that Max cared about him. Emma did, too. Talking to her mother had reminded Maddie how lucky she was to have a loving family. Jack had one and he was throwing it away. Not if she could help it.

"Mr Valentine, you have no idea what my duties entail and I'm not about to discuss it with you. Unlike Jack, I don't really care what you think of me. I'm not after your respect."

"That's quite clear." His tone was clipped.

"I simply felt that it was past time you knew the truth." She stood and gathered up her things.

"No offense, my dear, but I barely know you. Why in the world should I believe this preposterous story?"

She shrugged. "No reason except that it's the truth. The problem is that if you do believe, you'd have to admit you were wrong. And it cost you a lot of years with Jack. It's past time for you to stop being an idiot and be a father to your son."

Maddie walked out of the office in a haze and that didn't clear until she passed the table where she and Jack had had lunch on Boxing Day. The spot where she'd called him an idiot, too.

The very place she'd begun to fall in love.

Another couple sat there now and smiled into each other's eyes. They didn't notice anything around them, not even her standing and staring.

Or the tears trickling down her cheeks.

* * *

Maddie pushed the button for the elevator to take her up to the Durley House suite. She'd just called Jack's father an idiot and she wasn't sorry. Although she didn't think that mattered one way or the other since the man had shown very little emotion to her tirade on Jack's behalf.

She'd thought she would feel some sense of relief, but she simply felt drained. On top of that, she dreaded facing Jack after throwing herself at him the night before. He'd saved her the humiliation of "going all the way" but that was little comfort. In her frame of reference, humiliation was a campus full of college guys pointing and laughing because your virginity was the stakes in a fraternity bet. What she felt now was so much deeper. It was as if all the light in her world had just gone dark. It was as if the carrot of happiness always dangling just out of reach had suddenly disappeared forever.

She'd offered herself to Jack without considering marriage or long term. It was a principle she'd held dear, then compromised without a second thought because it was the simple, logical next step when one was hopelessly in love. In a weird way, she would almost feel better if she'd slept with Jack before he'd told her there couldn't be anything between them. Then she could hate him with all the force of this awful pain. But he'd stolen that from her too.

What a lousy time he'd picked to be noble.

The elevator doors whispered open and she stepped inside. For the first time ever, she wished it would get stuck. Put off the inevitable.

But it smoothly and efficiently carried her to the correct floor as expected of an elevator in a five-star hotel. She walked to the suite and opened the door. Jack was sitting at the coffee table with his open laptop in front of him.

He looked up. "I'm glad you're back."

Had he missed her? Hope sprang eternal… "Oh?" she asked as casually as possible.

"I've got a proposal that I'd like you to take a look at." He glanced down at the screen. "I know you've made up your mind, but this is a new and promising laser communications technology. The guy's been working on it a number of years but can't make significant progress without financial backing. I'll print out—"

"Don't bother."

Without taking off her coat, she walked into her bedroom and pulled her suitcase from the closet and started packing.

"What are you doing, Maddie?" Jack stood in the doorway.

She only sensed it, because she couldn't look at him. She'd cry and he wasn't worth it. How many hundreds of years would have to pass before that lie became the truth?

"Come on, Jack. You're brighter than the average bear. Surely you can see I'm packing."

"Why?"

"Because I'm going home." She threw several sweaters and a pair of jeans into the jumble of clothes.

"Why?"

Because she missed home. She missed her family. He was no longer the boss who teased and harmlessly flirted with her. That relationship was gone and she'd never get it back. Because he was the man she loved.

As soon as she'd walked in and looked at him the stab of pain had told her she couldn't go back to New York and pretend nothing had happened. She couldn't go into the office day after day and see him and know he would never return her feelings. The prospect of that was too grim to contemplate.

Now she did look at him. She pulled herself

together and looked into his bad-boy blue eyes and said, "I can't work for you any more."

"I see." The tone was cool, but his gaze turned hot and angry. He was looking at her the way he'd looked at his mother when she'd admitted asking the unthinkable of him had been wrong. "I suppose there's nothing I can say to change your mind?"

Not unless he could say he loved her and mean it. "No. Nothing."

He nodded, then turned away without another word. The second he disappeared, Maddie knew with a terrible certainty that her heart would never be whole again.

CHAPTER TEN

JACK prowled the suite at Durley House and brooded over the fact that not only *hadn't* Maddie thanked him in the morning, she'd quit.

Frustration twisted inside him, and not for the first time. A vision of the few moments she'd been in his bed slammed through him. She was so lovely in every way, inside and out. He'd wanted her then. The wanting was worse now, but nothing changed the fact that he didn't deserve her. Closing his eyes, he tried to shut out the hurt and humiliation on her face when she'd run from him. Yet he'd been stupid enough to believe she would thank him in the morning.

But she'd left.

Good riddance, he thought, deliberately fueling his anger. It was all he had.

There was a knock on the door and he was grateful for the welcome distraction, until he opened up and saw who it was.

"Dad."

"Jack." The old man smiled. "May I come in?"

"I don't think we have anything left to say." Jack really didn't need this. The way he'd treated Maddie, he'd lived up to his father's low expectations. Another round with the man who believed he could do nothing right wasn't high on his list.

But he heard Maddie's voice in his head saying his father loved him, preaching forgiveness. "Come in."

Robert walked past him and looked around the suite, nodding with satisfaction. "This is nice, Jack."

"I've been comfortable here." Maddie had liked it, he remembered. All their comforts had been taken care of with competent efficiency. The room service options—quiet delivery by private lift, or the personal touch of a proper, polite butler. He remembered her pleasure during Christmas dinner.

Speaking of polite, he should invite his father to sit, but he couldn't get the words out. "What do you want, Dad?"

Robert turned and met his gaze. "Maddie came to see me yesterday."

That stunned him, but it also explained where she'd been before coming back to give her notice. When he finally responded, all he could say was, "I can't imagine what she would have to say to you."

"Maddie decided it was time for me to know that I held you accountable for something you didn't do."

Jack had never told another soul. Not ever. He'd trusted Maddie as he'd never trusted another woman and shared his most personal emotions. And she took the information straight to the one man on earth who wasn't to know.

"Maddie had no right to tell you that," he ground out.

Robert slid his hands into the pockets of his slacks, lifting the bottom of the matching jacket. "Ease off, Jack. She was trying to help."

Help? Or punish him? "That was my mother's secret. She begged me to keep it from you."

His father looked thoughtful. "How is your mother?"

The question came from out of the blue and surprised Jack. "Not that you'd care, but she's fine. She and Aidan."

"Aidan? So she's not alone." Robert nodded thoughtfully. "I'm glad. Despite what you think, I do care. I was no good for her. Never made her happy."

In a vulnerable moment, Jack had told Maddie something private, something no one else knew. "Maddie's never betrayed me before."

"She didn't now, son. She's right. It's time I knew. Time to put it in the past where it belongs and forget."

Twelve years of being alone, cut off from the people he loved. Jack shook his head. "That's not possible."

"I probably deserve that."

"You were destroying my mother," Jack shot back.

Robert sighed. "I'd like to say you're wrong about that, but I can't. I was selfish. I hurt your mother."

"And I am my mother's son," he said bitterly.

"You're a good son, certainly not because of me. Obviously your mother is responsible for the man you turned out to be. But you're a grown man now, a gifted businessman in your own right. What would you do if an employee shirked an important responsibility and all the evidence you had said they didn't lift a finger to do the job?"

The dark memory of being caught between his parents twisted inside Jack. Having to choose his mother but desperately hoping his father would somehow know he'd tried his best. "It was as if you expected me to screw up."

"You gave me no facts to the contrary, never offered a word of explanation. What else was I to think?"

His father had a point, although under the same circumstances Jack knew he would make the same choice. "I had to protect her from you. And *that's* your fault."

"I wish I could say you're wrong." Robert nodded grimly. "Your mother did get her revenge. The failure was very public and cost the business a great deal of money. It was a long time before we regained the reputation that was lost." He met Jack's gaze. "But the worst was that it cost me you."

Jack struggled through years of bitterness and blame as he thought. "I did what I had to do."

Robert's smile was sad. "I would give anything to undo what happened and take back the things I said to you that night. If I'd been a better parent, if we'd been able to talk, you might have trusted me with the truth. I'd like the opportunity to try again, Jack. It's time I stopped acting like an idiot and started being a father."

Jack stared. "I've never heard you talk like that before."

"Your assistant is quite straightforward, isn't she?"

Maddie had said that to him? Good for her. "She says what's on her mind, yes."

"We could both take a lesson from her. And I hope it's not too late for us to work on our communication." Robert's gaze was direct and unwavering. "It's time I told you how proud I am of you, son."

Again Jack was stunned. The words tapped into a place that was dark and empty. Sarcasm, the verbal weapon he'd learned from Maddie, made him want to say, Who are you and what have you done with Robert Valentine? But all he managed was, "Oh?"

Robert nodded. "In my world, business came before family. I suppose because it came easily to me. But I'm a failure as a father. And relationships with women?" Robert shrugged. "I'm not good at those either."

"What tipped you off? Four marriages?" Jack said.

Robert's mouth twisted in a smile. Then he was serious. "It's cost me more than you'll ever know. Business is important. But love should come first."

"That's rich coming from you."

"Isn't it, though?" The man seemed unperturbed by the criticism. "If I'd put love first, I wouldn't have made so many mistakes. With Max. Emma." He met Jack's gaze directly. "With you especially."

Jack didn't know what to say. He'd held his anger and bitterness up as a shield for so long, he felt as if he had nowhere to hide. And Maddie was responsible for this mess.

"While this is all very interesting, Dad, none of it excuses the fact that Maddie went to you with information that wasn't hers to share."

"Don't be angry with her, Jack." Something in his father's eyes pleaded for understanding. "She did what she thought was for your own good, my boy. You know she's in love with you."

"You wouldn't know love if it came up and shook your hand."

"She defended you like a mother cat protecting her young."

"She did?"

"Quite. I have a feeling you love her, too." His look was thoughtful, as if he was remembering. "I loved a woman once, and only when she died did I realize how much I'd lost. Then it was too late. Don't make the same mistake, son. Tell Maddie how you feel before it's too late."

It's already too late, Jack thought. The fading glow of anger highlighted the awful truth. He'd ruined his chance with her.

Then he glanced at his father and the look on the man's face was something he'd never seen before. Pride. Love. Respect. Sadness. All the things Maddie had told him she'd seen in his father just from that short first meeting.

Jack had run from a lousy situation, but he

would never know what might have happened if he'd stayed. The loneliness of twelve years lashed him and he admitted something he'd been trying to ignore. He'd missed his family— all of them, including his father. If he didn't make it up now, there might never be another opportunity and he couldn't live with that regret.

Maddie had brought this about. Maddie was the voice in his head. She told him what she thought whether he wanted to hear it or not. She did what she thought was right and let the chips fall where they might. He respected her. He admired her. He needed her. He…

Damn his father for being right. He *was* in love with her.

"All right, Dad. I won't be angry with Maddie."

Robert nodded. "Good. Now then. Can we discuss you staying in London?"

"I'm not here permanently."

"In spite of your threat to dismantle it, I was

rather hoping you'd come back to stay and run the business."

Jack shook his head. "No. About the business… From what I've been able to gather, you and Uncle John are pulling it apart. Each trying to take control."

"I'm the logical choice. It's John's son who put us in this financial bind."

"Does it really matter now? The most important thing is to save Bella Lucia." Until this moment, Jack hadn't even realized he felt that way. Once the words were out, the feeling gained momentum. "The thing is, neither one of you is getting any younger. You need to think about retiring."

"If we do and you're not staying, who would run the restaurants?"

"Max is the logical choice. He's been there every step of the way. I'm waiting to see the business plan he's preparing for me." Jack didn't want to say anything yet, but with the capital he planned to invest the cash crisis wouldn't be an issue.

"You're sure you won't stay on?"

Jack shook his head. "My life isn't here any more, Dad."

The man actually looked disappointed and the fact that Jack could recognize the emotion was an amazing thing in itself. All thanks to Maddie.

"Of course." Robert's smile was sad. "But you can't blame a father for hoping."

The man was reaching out. Could he do any less than meet him halfway? Jack stuck out his hand. "I promise it won't be another twelve years. From now on I won't be a stranger here in London."

Robert took the hand, then pulled him close for a bear hug. It wasn't easy; it wasn't familiar. But the ice was broken.

Robert pulled back. "I'll look forward to seeing you again soon, then."

"Me, too." Jack smiled at his father, something he'd never believed he could do.

His mother had urged him to forgive, but Jack knew he wasn't quite there. Forgetting would be a disservice to both himself and his father and the progress they'd made today, but he was ready to leave the door open. He was ready to start the process of building a relationship with his dad.

The miracle of it could be laid directly at Maddie's feet.

Jack paced back and forth in the reception area at the solicitor's office. A lawyer's per-hour fee was stiff enough and he hoped there wouldn't be a charge for wearing out the thick green carpet. The walls were oak paneled and an information desk sat in the center of the large space. Glancing at his watch, for the umpteenth time, he hoped Max and Louise were on time. He'd ordered the plane to be ready for the flight back to New York. To Maddie. She wouldn't return his phone calls, so he would show up on her doorstep and camp there until he could make her listen.

The door opened and Louise Valentine walked in. A tall, athletic blonde with gray/blue eyes, she looked exceedingly professional in her power suit with the black skirt and red jacket. She glanced around and smiled when she saw him. "Hello, Jack."

"Lou. Thanks for coming."

She looked nervous. "What's going on?"

"I'll tell you when Max gets here."

"He's coming?" Her look said she'd rather be exposed to influenza.

"I called him and he agreed to be here."

Just then Max opened the door. He smiled at Jack, but when he saw Louise his expression became hooded. "Lou."

"Max," she said, coolly.

"Good. We're all here." Jack looked at his watch.

Max slid his hands into the pockets of his pin-striped slacks. "What are you up to, Jack? Why are we here?"

"I've decided to save the business, not take it apart," he explained, staring at Max. His brother nodded his understanding. "The solicitor is going to draw up the investment papers."

"Excellent news." Max grinned until his gaze landed on Louise. "But I don't understand why she's here."

"It's nice to see you, too," she said.

"That's why." Jack glanced between the two of them. "This family is tearing itself apart and I'm not going to let it happen. You're each here as a representative from the warring factions."

Louise settled the strap of her small black leather purse more securely on her shoulder. "What are you? The family fairy godmother?"

Jack grinned. "In a manner of speaking."

"When did this transformation come about?" Max demanded.

"I'm still a work in progress," Jack admitted. "I guess you could say Emma started it and Maddie nursed it along." He met his brother's gaze. "I saw Dad and we got things out in the open."

"I see." Max's tone said he didn't see at all.

"I've missed family. I didn't realize how much until coming back. You guys don't appreciate it because it's right here in front of you." Not unlike him and Maddie. He hadn't fully recognized the value of what he shared with her until she'd left. But he would fix that. First things first. "I'm going to bail out the restaurants, but both sides of the family have to work together to be successful." He looked at Max. "I think your first order of business should be to hire Louise."

His two companions exchanged a stunned look.

"Why?" Max asked.

Jack slid his hands into the pockets of his slacks. "She's a gifted PR and marketing consultant who can give you exactly the right kind of support. I saw her in action at Emma's embassy party and it seemed she wasn't intimidated by the rich, famous, powerful or royalty."

"But—"

"Really, Max." Louise glared at him. "Don't look so shocked. I'm not without skills."

"Let me remind you in case you've forgotten," Max said. "We tried working together. It was a disaster."

"He fired me," Louise explained to Jack.

"Ah." Jack studied the two of them and had the feeling that there was more to it. If he'd learned anything, it was that there were two sides to every story. They would have to work it out.

"Then you should rehire her," Jack persisted. "This family needs to learn to work together."

"What made you decide to put the money into Bella Lucia?" Louise asked.

Max slid her a look, then shook his head as if she were a bit slow. "It was because of Maddie."

"The woman who came to the Christmas party with you?" When Max snorted, Louise glared at Max. "Don't even go there again. I don't want to hear about my outfit."

"You mean the fuzzy white crop top, short red suede skirt with boots? Oh, and the flashing mistletoe belly-button jewelry? It never crossed my mind," Max said.

"That was Christmas," Louise huffed. "You should be able to express yourself with your family."

"My point exactly," Jack said. He remembered his spur-of-the-moment decision to bring Maddie with him to London. Now he realized that he'd known she would be his bridge back to his family.

"Maddie had a lot to do with my decision,"

he admitted. "And you, Max. The business plan is brilliant—"

"Oh, please," Louise interrupted. "Don't feed his already inflated ego."

Jack studied his cousin Louise and couldn't help comparing her to Maddie although the two looked nothing alike. His cousin's air of confident businesswoman and her sassy comebacks reminded him of Maddie. And when Max and Lou exchanged a look filled with sparks, Jack wondered about their relationship. He had a feeling it would be electric, not unlike his with Maddie. God, he missed her.

"Where is Maddie?" Max asked, as if he could read thoughts. "I expected to see her here."

"No." Jack felt her absence as if half of himself were missing. "She left for New York a couple days ago."

"Did you two have a problem?" Max asked, studying him closely.

"We had a—" His brother knew him too well. There was no point in glossing over the truth. "The problem is I was a jerk."

Sympathy brimmed in her eyes as Louise patted his arm. "Recognizing the problem is halfway to solving it, Jack. A bit of groveling wouldn't hurt either."

"A lot you know," Max scoffed.

"I know more than you think," she shot back, before meeting Jack's gaze again. "Is your business here in London finished, then?"

Jack nodded. "As soon as we see the solicitor, I'm heading back to New York."

"Give Maddie my regards," Max said.

"I'll do that." Jack was no longer jealous of his brother. Maddie had been waiting to give herself to the man she loved and wouldn't have come to Jack's bed unless she'd had deep feelings for him. Hopefully he hadn't crushed that out of her because he was counting on the fact that she still cared to win her back.

"Good luck," Max added.

Jack would need every bit of luck and all the charm he could muster. He had to believe it wasn't too late for him and Maddie. He'd faced the fact that he was his father's son, but that didn't mean he couldn't learn from his mistakes.

Jack had found the woman he wanted, the only woman in the world who could make him happy. And she'd been right under his nose all the time.

No matter how long it took, no matter what he had to do, he would convince Maddie that they should be together.

CHAPTER ELEVEN

A PLEASANT late-afternoon breeze drifted over Maddie as she sat on a lounge chair in the garden at the Hotel Villa Medici, sipping a full-bodied Cabernet. They said red wine was good for a person's heart and she was putting the theory to the test. Granted, she'd only taken a couple of sips, but she didn't feel better. She missed Jack and her heart ached with it.

That wasn't all. She missed her job at Valentine Ventures and hated that hindsight was twenty/twenty. She should never have gone to London. That trip, plus a jaunt to

Ireland with some hot kisses in Jack's bed all added up to her worst nightmare. She'd had to quit the job she loved because she dreaded seeing the boss she loved.

On the upside, the generous salary from that job had allowed her to fulfill her dream of coming to Florence. It had been her mother's suggestion after Maddie had unburdened herself. She'd thought it a good idea and quickly made reservations. She'd just barely checked into her lovely room when she realized she could fly around the world, but she couldn't run away from her problems.

"Hello, Maddie."

At the deep, familiar voice, the hairs on the back of her neck prickled and every nerve ending in her body tingled with awareness. She looked up and put a hand up to shield her eyes from the glare of the setting sun. Speaking of problems... Jack stood in front of her and she wasn't completely certain he wasn't a figment of her imagination.

"Jack?"

"Maddie, I need to talk to you."

He'd followed her to Italy? "How did you know where to find me?"

"I talked to your mother when you didn't return my calls." He indicated the padded wrought-iron lounge beside her. "Do you mind if I sit down?"

"And if I do?" He'd followed her to Italy? She couldn't seem to get past that.

"It's important."

"I'm pretty busy," she said coolly, although her heart was skipping like a stone over water.

"I can see," he said wryly. "Please."

Had reckless Jack Valentine ever said please? She couldn't remember. More important, she couldn't turn him down. He'd come all the way to Italy. She took a deep, cleansing breath and braced herself to get this over with. She told herself it was like jumping into frigid water—the first sensation was bitter cold and shocking, then you got used to it. Then you could deal with it.

She couldn't backspace her life and delete her mistake, but she would do her darnedest to forget that anything personal had happened between them.

"Okay."

He sat on the lounge, but didn't stretch out. There wasn't a lot of space for his long legs between the chaises and his knees were only inches from her thigh. Was it her imagination, or could she actually feel the warmth of his body?

Was it true what they said about absence making the heart grow fonder? Because he looked better than any man had a right to look. His dark hair was artfully mussed and sexy as sin. His expensively worn jeans molded to muscular thighs and the long sleeves of his shirt were rolled up to just below his elbows. The light blue color brought out the scoundrel in his eyes.

It would be so much easier to resist him if he'd had the decency to wear a suit and tie, except that wasn't Jack. And this was Italy.

"What do you want, Jack?"

He reached out, as if to touch her, then rested his forearms on his thighs. "It's good to see you, Maddie."

"It's only been a week." It felt so much longer.

"Ten days," he corrected.

It felt like a lifetime. "Okay."

"I understand you visited my father."

Her gaze snapped to his. "How did you know?"

"He came to see me."

Something darkened in his eyes and she got a bad feeling. Her decision to see Robert Valentine had been impulsive; she hadn't really thought about the ramifications. Someone had needed to mediate. She'd just gone with her gut; it was what Jack would have done. But what if she'd made things worse? And she couldn't tell whether or not Jack was angry. Not that it mattered. What was he going to do? Fire her? She didn't work for him any more.

"How did it go?" she asked, studying him, waiting for the intensity that mention of his father always generated.

He linked his fingers together. "It was… interesting."

That wasn't very helpful. She didn't want to be curious, but she couldn't seem to help it where Jack was concerned. "Would you care to elaborate?"

"He explained things from his perspective. I told him why I did what I did. He apologized and said it was time he stopped acting like an idiot and started being a father."

Maddie stared at him. "He said that?"

"He did." The corners of Jack's wonderful

mouth turned up and she knew he knew she'd said it. "Dad and I are going to work on our communication."

"I'm glad, Jack. What about your mother?"

"I called to apologize for my abrupt exit. We talked and things there are on the mend, too."

Inside, Maddie was doing the dance of joy. It was good that he'd patched up things with his family. At least that part of the trip had been successful.

"That's good. What about Bella Lucia?" Beautiful Lucy, the business begun because of a man's love for a woman. The thought made her heart ache because it wasn't likely a man would ever love her that much. The only man she wanted was Jack and he'd made it clear how he felt.

"Before leaving London I made arrangements to infuse the restaurants with the capital necessary to keep them running and get the family business healthy again. Max is going to take over."

"I'm so glad, Jack."

He nodded. "I thought you'd approve."

"I do. You did a good thing. I'm sure your family is very grateful. They must be—" She forgot herself and leaned forward to touch him, then froze.

"What?"

"Nothing." She dropped her hand. This was why she'd quit. She couldn't keep her feelings from showing. "Why did you come all the way to Florence?"

"I want to talk about us."

Just like that his intensity was back. All that focus directed at her was unexpectedly sexy and stole the air from her lungs.

She sat up straighter. "There is no 'us'. I'm sorry you came all this way to talk about nothing."

"I have plenty to say."

"I can't imagine what."

"First, I want you to come back to work for me."

She swung her legs to the side and sat up straight, facing him. After setting her wine on the glass-topped table beside her, she said, "I told you why I can't do that."

"Because of what I said—that there can't be anything more than business between us."

How like Jack to surprise her. He was taking responsibility. "Give the man a gold star."

"I was wrong about that. I love you, Maddie."

"I don't believe you." She stood up and backed away.

"Don't look so shocked."

She didn't know how else to look. "You can't be serious."

"Dead serious," he answered.

"I guess on a professional, career level I should be flattered. Apparently you'll go to any lengths to keep me from quitting."

"I love you," he said, an edge to his voice.

"Oh, please. I bet you say that to all the girls to get what you want. The problem is that you've made it clear to me what you *don't* want—in a word, marriage and family."

"That's two words," he pointed out far too rationally.

"Whatever. It's a deal breaker for me." She'd had enough of him taunting her with the only words that could rip her heart out. Her eyes burned and it took every ounce of her control to keep back the tears. She stood. "You'll never change, Jack."

He loved her? What had made him say that? She'd told him once that she was waiting for love. Correction: someone to love her. He was using her words against her. Why?

"You're wrong, Maddie." Before she could walk away, he stood and took her arm.

He was far stronger than she and the grip was

impossible to break without struggling, if then. "You hurt me, Jack. You threw my feelings back in my face and, unlike your other disposable women, I didn't even get flowers. Why in the world would I set myself up for that again? And why would you bother? The world is full of women who would be happy to play your game." She looked at his fingers on her arm, then glared.

Jack dropped his hand. "I'm not playing anything."

"Neither am I," she said and walked away.

His voice drifted to her. "We're not through, Maddie. I'll be back."

"To Bella Lucia," Jack said and touched his glass to Max's.

"Cheers." Max grinned, then sipped his wine. "It's just like old times. Except for the fact that you just saved the Valentine family's skin."

The two of them were sitting at a table in a pub around the corner from the solicitor's office where Jack had just signed the paperwork giving him a controlling interest in the family company. It was like old times and Jack experienced a contentment he hadn't known in a long while—if ever.

"How does it feel?" Max asked.

"Pretty damn good." And Maddie was responsible. She made him want to be a better man and part of that was doing the right thing by his family. The legal business with his family couldn't wait, which was why he'd taken this quick trip to London. That and Maddie needed some time to think about what he'd said. He was the doer and she was the thinker, which was why they were so good together.

Jack raised his glass again. "To the new head of the Bella Lucia restaurants."

"Who would that be?" Max asked.

Jack grinned. "You."

"Me?" His brother looked surprised. "You're sure about that?"

"I am, yes. Unless you think you can't handle it?" Jack teased.

"Try and stop me," Max scoffed. "My only reservations are Dad and Uncle John. Neither will gracefully take a back seat after wrestling so bitterly for control of the company."

"It's time the two of them retired," Jack said. "And they *will* retire. You'll be in charge. I promise."

"Excellent news." Max grinned. "I've been impatient to move the company into the twenty-first century for some time now."

"What do you have in mind?"

"Expansion," Max said. "I've been meeting quietly with a friend of mine from Eton— Sheikh Surim."

"How very James Bond of you."

"Yes, well. He has quite a lucrative tourist resort in the desert kingdom of Qu'Arim. And he's receptive to the idea of opening a branch of Bella Lucia there."

"I see."

Max leaned forward eagerly. "Jack, have you any idea how big this is?"

"How big?"

"It could be the first step in making the Bella Lucia empire global."

"That's big." Jack grinned.

Max looked annoyed. "Oh, buzz off."

"No, seriously."

"Seriously," his brother said. "You and I are in this together and it does feel good."

Jack could feel his brother's excitement and shared it—to a point. "I'm in this, Max, but not quite together. It's your baby now, not mine."

"What are you saying?"

That he wouldn't make his father's mistakes. "I don't want an active role. I intend to have a life."

Max studied him intently. "Would a certain beautiful blonde named Maddie have anything to do with that decision?"

"Am I that easy to read?"

"Yes."

Jack needed Maddie to believe he was telling the truth about loving her. He hadn't been this nervous since—well, never. Not even when he'd wagered everything he had into a computer software deal. He had more than money at stake now. "I've mended fences with family and I need to do the same with her. It won't be easy. I just left her in Florence and she was pretty adamant about not giving me a chance."

"Persistence, old chap. It works in business and romance."

"I hope you're right." She'd looked angry and hurt. That was a formidable combination even for persistence. Although Jack didn't have any plans to give up. Ever.

"Would I steer you wrong? Didn't I teach you everything you know about women?" Max grinned.

"That's what I'm afraid of." Jack teased, but he was raw with nerves. If Maddie wouldn't have him…

"Just tell her what's in your heart and it will be fine. I wish you all the luck," Max said. "And every happiness."

Jack knew he'd need every bit of luck he could get. Then he heard Maddie's voice in his head. He didn't have to work to prove himself; he had to work to be happy. And he'd work the rest of his life to make her happy, too.

CHAPTER TWELVE

FOR as long as she could remember, Maddie had dreamed of seeing Florence, but her dreams had never included seeing the beautiful city alone. And she hadn't realized that part until Jack had shown up.

Pain sliced through her and it was all his fault. He was irritating and sweet in equal parts. Tracking her down. Pleading his case. Then disappearing. Actually, she'd walked away, but he'd said he would see her again and he hadn't shown up all day. What was he playing at? And no matter what he said, she couldn't afford to believe this wasn't a game to him. But a part of her couldn't reconcile the fact that he'd come all the way to Florence to see her. It was nothing more than a man who wasn't used to taking no for an answer.

Now she was in the back of a car riding through the city thanks to the hotel's outstanding customer service. Just because her room-service breakfast had been late, they'd insisted on making it up to her with dinner at one of Florence's most highly recommended restaurants. As they drove she looked at the buildings—historic churches and their ornate architecture, statues, *palazzos* and *piazzas*. All dressed up in bright lights.

It was everything she'd expected it would be and yet she'd never experienced quite this depth of loneliness. She didn't know where Jack was, but she carried him with her in her memories. Everywhere she looked there were reminders of him. The hotel suite—the last time she'd stayed in one, he'd been with her. Having a car and driver at her disposal was a Jack Valentine touch. Though she'd tried to protect herself from the type of men who were bad for her, she'd fallen for the rogue who'd been right in front of her.

"At least I'll always have Florence," she said softly as the car turned into a lot.

She looked at the white building with the red-tiled roof. In the distance was a panoramic view with the lights of Florence and the Arno valley that took her breath away. The sight distracted her for several moments and she didn't immediately realize that the parking lot was deserted.

Maddie sat forward and said to the driver, "Paolo, are you sure this is the right place?"

"*Sì*," he said in his heavy accent. He was a very handsome, thirtyish Italian with all the charm Italian men were reputed to have. "The hotel concierge personally gave me the address. This is Carpe Diem."

"Seize the day," she whispered. The name reminded her of Jack.

Paolo opened her door. "Shall I go in with you, miss?"

"I'll be fine." She slid out. "But it doesn't look like the place is open so I'd appreciate it if you wouldn't leave."

"Never," he vowed. When he grinned, his teeth were very white against his olive skin. "I am happy to drive such a beautiful lady."

He was charming; she was immune. And this was weird. It was time to find out what was going on. She expected to find the restaurant door locked, but when Paolo pulled it swung open easily.

Inside, the dark-haired, dark-eyed hostess in the chocolate-brown jersey dress smiled. "Miss Ford, I am Sophia."

"How did you know who I am?"

"The hotel told us to expect you."

It was dinner time at one of the city's top restaurants, yet the place seemed empty. "Where is everyone?"

Sophia's smile was friendly. "Follow me."

Maddie followed through the dimly lit corridor and several arched doorways. Somewhere there was a fountain and the trickling sounds drifted to her. The scent of flowers permeated everything and the sheer romantic ambience tugged at her.

The hostess stopped beside a table set only for two, covered with silverware, white linen, and a crystal vase containing a single red rose.

Maddie turned to Sophia. "I don't understand—"

"Hello, Maddie."

It was déjà vu. She whirled around—heart pounding. "Jack!"

He smiled at the young Italian woman. "Thank you, Sophia. I'll take it from here."

When they were alone, Maddie glared at him. "What's going on? You disappear without a word, then scare the wits out of me."

"I didn't mean to." He picked up the open bottle of wine on the table and poured some into the two glasses. "Let's drink to Florence—the city, not a person."

With the words came memories of Christmas in London and a whole lot of pain. "No."

He slid his hands into the pockets of his dark slacks. The cream-colored knit sweater high-lighted the contours of his wide chest. "All right. Then, tell me what tourist attractions you've seen so far."

She was about to tell him what he could do with his tourist attractions, then thought better of it. If she knew anything about Jack, it was that he was stubborn. She would get this over with quicker if she went along with his program.

"I've seen the Piazzale Michelangelo with its reproductions of the Medici chapel statues from San Lorenzo and Michelangelo's David. I toured the Ponte Vecchio, which is a wonderful bridge that was the only one spared by the retreating Germans at the end of World War II. I saw Santa Maria del Fiore and the Duomo, which dominates the skyline of the city." She stopped to take a breath.

"So you've been busy in my absence," he commented. "Is the city everything you hoped it would be?"

No. And that was all his fault. He'd taken the joy out of her world and she didn't know how to get it back. "It's a beautiful city."

His eyes darkened. "Not as beautiful as you."

"Let's cut to the chase, Jack. Why is the restaurant empty?"

"I reserved it for our private use. And before you ask, I did conspire with the hotel concierge to get you here. I wanted to surprise you."

Maddie knew he wasn't mean-spirited and couldn't imagine what reason he could possibly have for tricking her. "Why go to so much trouble?"

"Because I have a lot riding on what happens." His eyes locked on hers until heat settled low in her belly.

"Such as?" Her voice was a raspy whisper that had nothing to do with the echo in the deserted restaurant.

"My life and happiness." He took her hands in his warm ones and glanced at the rosebud. "This time I don't want to end with flowers. I want to signify the beginning of our relationship. It's a single red rose, a single everlasting love. Despite what you believe, I've never said this to any other woman. I love you, Maddie. I want to marry you."

She didn't get it. He'd had his chance and sent her away.

"Just so we're clear, I fell into your bed once, but it won't happen again."

He dropped her hands. "That's not what this is about."

"No? What other reason could you have for showing up here and using the L-word? And the M-word."

"I suppose I deserve that." His mouth thinned for a moment. "And, yes, I want you in my bed. I want you now as much as I wanted you when we were in Ireland. But it's more than sex, Maddie. I want you in my life. I want to have children with you. I want us to grow old together. I want to make you happy."

She couldn't take it all in and seized on the first thing he'd said. "You wanted me then?"

"Innocent, Maddie." His smile was fleeting as he tucked her hair behind her ear. "You have no idea how hard it was for me to let you go that night."

"Then why did you?"

"Because you shocked the hell out of me when you dropped the bombshell that it was your first time. Because you are an awesome responsibility and a profound gift. Because I'm not good enough for you."

For so long he'd wandered around alone and scared and trying to prove to his father that he wasn't a loser. It was time he started believing in himself. "I don't ever want to hear that again, Jack. You're a good and decent man."

"Not good enough for you." He let out a breath. "If I were, I'd walk away right now. But I can't do it, Maddie. I *need* you."

"You're not talking about business."

"That's the last thing I want to talk about," he said angrily. "This is very personal. I realized after you quit and left me in London that I've been in love with you for a very long time."

Maddie had seen the many faces of Jack Valentine—from charming to tormented—but never this desperation. She could hardly believe—was afraid to believe—this wasn't a wonderful dream. "If this is a line—"

Anger flashed through his eyes again, turning them dark blue. "I'm not being smooth or charming. I don't have the reserves left to pull that off. Besides, it wouldn't work because you'd see right through me."

That was true. And this angry Jack convinced her more surely of his sincerity than charm or smoothness could have done.

Jack shoved his fingers through his hair. "I'm simply stating the honest truth of my feelings. I love you and I want to marry you. And I won't settle for less. No compromises."

"You really do understand me."

"No man could ever love you the way I love you. No man could possibly love you more than I do and will for as long as I live. You're perfect for me." He cupped her face in his palms and his gaze captured and held her own. "You have every right to torture me, but I know you love me."

"You do?"

Tension rolled from him in waves. "You were ready to give yourself to me. I've never respected a woman more than I do you. You have expectations that I find myself wanting to meet. If I hadn't been so stupid and clumsy… I'd give up everything I own to take back the hurt I caused you, Maddie. Give me a chance. Let me make it up to you."

She smiled at him as happiness surged through her. "You already have, Jack. And you're right. I'm in love with you. I love you with all my heart."

He closed his eyes for a moment, and when he opened them his gaze was clear and carefree and…happy. "This is the most important venture of my life and I want to do it right." He went down on one knee as he dug in his pocket and pulled out a ring with the biggest diamond she'd ever seen. "Madison Ford, will you marry me?"

"Yes."

"Will you marry me here? In Florence? And let me take you on a honeymoon in the city you always wanted to see?"

"Yes," she whispered.

Maddie had never really believed it possible that she could have everything she ever wanted and still stay true to herself. But when Jack stood and took her in his arms, then settled his lips on hers, she knew her bad-boy boss would make all her dreams come true.

MILLS & BOON® PUBLISH EIGHT LARGE PRINT TITLES A MONTH. THESE ARE THE EIGHT TITLES FOR APRIL 2007

———————— ❦ ————————

THE CHRISTMAS BRIDE
Penny Jordan

RELUCTANT MISTRESS, BLACKMAILED WIFE
Lynne Graham

AT THE GREEK TYCOON'S PLEASURE
Cathy Williams

THE VIRGIN'S PRICE
Melanie Milburne

THE BRIDE OF MONTEFALCO
Rebecca Winters

CRAZY ABOUT THE BOSS
Teresa Southwick

CLAIMING THE CATTLEMAN'S HEART
Barbara Hannay

BLIND-DATE MARRIAGE
Fiona Harper

MILLS & BOON®

Live the emotion

0307 Rom LP

MILLS & BOON® PUBLISH EIGHT LARGE PRINT TITLES A MONTH. THESE ARE THE EIGHT TITLES FOR MAY 2007

❦

THE ITALIAN'S FUTURE BRIDE
Michelle Reid

PLEASURED IN THE BILLIONAIRE'S BED
Miranda Lee

BLACKMAILED BY DIAMONDS, BOUND BY MARRIAGE
Sarah Morgan

THE GREEK BOSS'S BRIDE
Chantelle Shaw

OUTBACK MAN SEEKS WIFE
Margaret Way

THE NANNY AND THE SHEIKH
Barbara McMahon

THE BUSINESSMAN'S BRIDE
Jackie Braun

MEANT-TO-BE MOTHER
Ally Blake

MILLS & BOON®